D1606020

The Island of the Dead

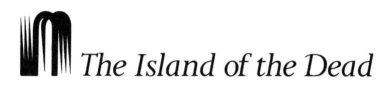 *The Island of the Dead*

LYA LUFT

Translated by

CARMEN CHAVES MCCLENDON

and

BETTY JEAN CRAIGE

The University of Georgia Press

Athens and London

O Quarto Fechado © 1984 by Lya Luft
The Island of the Dead © 1986 by Lya Luft
Published in 1986 by the University of Georgia Press
Athens, Georgia 30602

Designed by Kathi L. Dailey
Set in 10 on 13 Linotron 202 Merganthaler Pilgrim
The paper in this book meets the guidelines for
permanence and durability of the Committee on
Production Guidelines for Book Longevity of the
Council on Library Resources

Printed in the United States of America

90 89 88 87 86   5 4 3 2 1

Library of Congress Cataloging in Publication Data

Luft, Lya Fett.
   The island of the dead.

   Translation of: O quarto fechado.
   I. Title.
PQ9698.22.U3Q3713   1986   869.3   85-24527
ISBN 0-8203-0836-6

To Karen and Kristi McClendon

Contents

Translators' Preface

I am a translator myself, for twenty years now . . .
[and] as a writer I also know how much has to be done
to translate any book, because each sentence, each
word, was chosen by the writer [for] its particular music, its secret meanings, etc.

—LYA LUFT

Translator, poet, and essayist, Lya Luft was no
stranger to Brazilian literary circles when she published her
first novel, *As Parceiras*, in 1980. As a translator from Ger-
man and English into Portuguese, Luft has published more
than fifty works in Brazil by such authors as Virginia Woolf,
Thomas Mann, Robert Musil, Rainer Maria Rilke, Gunter
Grass, and Norman Mailer. As a poet, she has published
three volumes, *Canções de Limiar* (1963), *Flauta Doce*
(1972), and *Mulher no Palco* (1984). As an essayist, she has
published a weekly column in *Correio do Povo*, the oldest
daily newspaper in Porto Alegre, where she lives, and a col-
lection of essays, *Matéria do Cotidiano* (1978). And now as a
novelist she has produced, in addition to *As Parceiras*, *A Asa
Esquerda do Anjo* (1981), *Reunião de Familia* (1982), and *O*

Quarto Fechado (1984), which we have translated as *The Island of the Dead*.

The Island of the Dead (whose title in Portuguese means literally "The Closed Room") is what Luft calls one of her studies of "closed family relationships"; it is an analysis of family members' emotional struggles with self-disclosure in the face of a child's death. In this novel no omniscient narrator mediates between the characters and the reader to inform us of what has really happened or to allow us to escape the claustrophobic confinement of the characters' thought and speech. The action, taking place during a wake for an eighteen-year-old boy named Camilo who has taken his own life, consists almost entirely of the thoughts of the family members: the boy's mother, Renata, who has given up a career as a concert pianist for marriage and motherhood; his father, Martin; his maiden aunt, Clara; his foster grandmother (whom they call "Mother"); and his twin sister, Carolina. The point of view shifts from one mind to another, back and forth, as the characters, through their separate memories, together reconstruct the boy's past. Even the dead boy takes part, in sections headed by the phrase, "If he could speak the dead boy would say . . ."

Early in the novel Renata reveals her fascination with a reproduction of Böcklin's *Island of the Dead*, which as a child she had on the wall over her piano. Now, as she gazes at the casket in the middle of the room, the casket holding her son, she thinks of the painting and wonders who that white-robed figure might be who stands in the prow of a boat taking a casket across still waters to the Island of the Dead. The painting becomes the source of a metaphorical elaboration on the nature of death, evoked by Renata's questions, "Where is Camilo?" and "What is . . . Death?"

As each of the characters explores the past, always with the question of how Camilo came to kill himself, the reader becomes aware of another figure in the family's history. It is

Mother's illegitimate daughter, Martin's cousin, who because of an accident that paralyzed her long ago has rotted in "the closed room" for thirty years as a huge mass of flesh, unable to speak, attended by Mother.

This creature, repulsive yet fascinating to every member of the family, is Ella, the only character in the novel whose point of view is not represented. Her name carries a strangeness to the Brazilian reader, who hears the word *Ella* as *ela*, or "she," but it loses the ambiguity for the American reader, for whom "Ella" is a first name. "Ella," says Martin. "Who would have chosen for the fatherless girl a name so ambiguous, so prophetic, of half humanity and half absence?" And Ella the character is both present and absent, present as a particular human being whose enormous body no longer functions properly and absent as the person her family once knew: she no longer speaks or even appears to be conscious.

Ella's name is ambiguous in another sense, in that Luft's identification of the character Ella with the personal pronoun *ela* allows the identification, central to the novel's theme, of Ella/*Ela* with Death, personified as a woman. Because the gender of the noun *morte* ("death") is feminine in Portuguese, Luft refers to death with the pronoun *ela* from the beginning of the novel, naturally. But it is not natural, however, to use the pronoun "she" to signify "death" in English. As translators we had to decide whether to hide the personification of death early in the novel by using the word "it" or to make obvious the personification to the American reader for whom the word "she" would be out of place. We attempted a compromise, avoiding the use of the pronoun when possible early and then using the pronoun "she" later when the personification becomes more evident. We could find no way in English to conflate Ella's name with the personal pronoun "she," and therefore we lose the hints given in the Brazilian original that "Death" is *Ela*/Ella.

If we believe that different readers read the same text

differently, as we now do in our relativist world, then we can see that there is no possibility of reproducing for the translators' culture the relationship of the Brazilian reader to the Brazilian novel. The two texts are in two different languages; the two languages embody two distinct ways of constructing reality; and within each of the two cultures no two readers read alike. We have, nevertheless, attempted to produce a close translation of Luft's novel to make the American reader aware of the strangeness of the original text and to bring across some of its "secret meanings."

Acknowledgments

We thank James B. Colvert for his careful reading of the manuscript for its style, and we thank Lya Luft and Alexandrino Severino for their careful reading of the manuscript for its accuracy. It was a pleasure to work with them.

The Island of the Dead

First Part: The Island

When we think that we are inside of life, Death begins
to weep inside of us.

RILKE

I

He took the first steps in his Death, embraced by Death, who instructed him slowly. There was no hurry. He drifted away, slowly, haltingly, departing a world which interested him no longer. He had the face of an adolescent, delicate, almost the face of a woman. But dusted lightly with gold, its youth lost and replaced by that solemn mask of wax, ice, and new knowledge.

Nothing bothered him—not voices, not discreet coughs, not doors opening and closing, not the people who approached, curious, confused, disturbed. He was dead, immune even to the flow of emotions circulating between the man and the woman seated on either side of the casket. Hardly speaking to each other, they felt exposed, ugly, naked. The pain they shared in public united them in an intimacy they no longer desired.

With pain and bewilderment rising from the depths of

their bowels, they were at the point of screaming, "What *is* that thing called Death?"

But they remained calm, trying to ignore each other.

The woman seemed very tired, her fingers moved from time to time on her lap, as if fingering an imaginary keyboard. Her husband, however, appeared tense, as if he might momentarily rise from the chair with clenched fists to batter the bony chest of Death, who, without his permission, was ruling his house.

The few people keeping watch over the body at that hour sat in chairs along the walls of the room, the furniture having been removed to make space. Those leaving the house frowned and turned up their collars before plunging into a world obliterated by fog. The fog had arrived stealthily. It stuck to the house, tried to enter, and wound around the plants and the people, insistent and desperate.

And yet, leaving the house, they would each breathe deeply of the damp air. It was better than the air inside, which reeked of death, candles, flowers, and suffering bodies.

Those who stayed in the room were almost faint with exhaustion, cold, and discomfort. Cigarette smoke formed clouds under the chandelier, as in false theater scenery. Someone yawned periodically without bothering to hide it.

In the middle of the room, on metal legs hidden by the shadows, the casket and its passenger floated on dark waters.

The father, sitting beside it, stretched his legs in search of a more comfortable position, and then drew them back again, embarrassed at still being able to move. He was an energetic man, but insecure in death's territory. He wanted to cry, rebel, act.

Who was his Adversary? Deceptive, transparent shadows, that only pretend to let themselves be pierced—they were everywhere and nowhere.

From the other bank, Renata surreptitiously observed

6

her husband. Her ex-husband, the man whom she had loved, Martin. She knew by heart every crease in his face, every detail and secret of his body. The bitterness, the disillusionment of the present had not distorted the features she had loved when she was young.

She had lived with him, slept with him, for many years, and had made him suffer. With him she had gone from ecstasy to alienation, from passion to hatred, and with him she had seen disintegrate what they had built to last forever. But an interior gulf had never been overcome. Ardor and sweetness had turned to impatience, after being lovers they had become strangers. Whose fault was it?

A successful pianist, Renata had come down from the concert stage to Martin's world, a matter-of-fact world of strength and rationality. But old enough to have her habits already ingrained, she hadn't been able to change. She had tried to substitute her domestic life for her art, but very soon found her new surroundings vulgar. Until then she had concentrated on herself, she could not share herself with another. With so many demands on her now, she felt impotent.

No, love had not been enough. They had gone through all the stages of a slow, painful separation. They rarely saw each other; actually they avoided each other, fearing new scenes.

Years ago she had said, "I'm not the type to get married," seeing women her age surrounded by children. After marriage, too late, she realized that she had been right. Even though it could be lonely, difficult, and sterile, her art was less complex for her than human love.

I loved you as much as I could love, she thought, trying not to look at Martin. Plans, dreams, all undone like a wax figure come near a flame, everything melts, beauty turns to caricature.

Their children, instead of creating ties, brought separation, and became problems themselves. That night beside the corpse, the two parents shared their grief, strangled as they were by the same silent cry: "What have I done to you, my son?"

I have never loved another woman the way I loved her, Martin thought. I have had so many women—women who were prettier, more jovial, more sensual—but she tormented me, and she means more to me than all the others.

He was embarrassed. Renata had been his weakness, his humiliation. At first he had thought he was strong, he would teach her about life and conquer her inner world, which attracted him so much. But he had been unable to do so. What was special in her was inaccessible to a man like Martin. However much he loved her, he needed something more— understanding, communication. Martin felt that their living together had made him constantly uncomfortable. She observes me, he thought, she analyzes me, and doesn't approve of me.

She was a stranger in his house, at his table, in his bed. He could sleep with her, but the more he tried to enter her soul the more they drew apart. Everything became caught up in blood and tears. Even if they had wanted to, they could no longer untangle themselves from that web. Renata was unstable, sometimes affectionate, then cold and mean to him, doing all she could to hurt him.

"I always end up hurting the people I love," she once confessed, crying. But more and more she isolated herself.

Even in their relationship with their dead son they were helpless. If they wanted to love him now, as they hadn't before, if they wanted to understand him, no matter how quiet and defenseless he might be, it would be like knocking on the door of a locked room whose key nobody has, not even its new tenant.

The waiting was torture for Martin. If only he could get out, run away, do something. He sighed, uncrossed his hands,

8

crossed them again on his lap. Conspicuous in the light for a moment, they looked powerful.

Renata saw them and was unable to escape the flood of memories.

"You have the hands of a pianist," she had said one day, passionately kissing his fingers, palms, wrists.

"But I'm not one of your delicate friends," Martin had answered seriously. "I'm basically a country man, don't fool yourself. A brute who is going to marry a goddess," he added laughing. And he gently squeezed her small head between his palms, running his fingers through her curly hair. "I can crush a goddess with these hands."

Renata kept her eyes wide open, to scare away the fatigue and the memories which threatened to overwhelm her, after hours of sitting there. She turned her attention to the painting at the stairs' landing. Now that night was falling and people had stopped coming by to embrace her and question her about the details of the death, she had plenty of time to ponder her favorite painting once more, now in a different light. Was it a castle? A prison? A small deserted dock. Ever since childhood, when the painting dominated the living room of her parents' house, she had wanted to know what it was all about.

Do all the dead go to a place like that? A fantastic painting. It was unreal to imagine that while this Island could exist, people continued walking and talking, women kept on cooking, children kept on going to school. The painting was much more fascinating to her than her daily routine, it was haunting, alluring.

As a child, she would stand in front of the canvas and think: Some day I'll get on that boat.

"How morbid!" her mother would say, pulling her away from it. "It's not for little girls to look at." The Island was gloomy and seductive, painted many years ago by a friend of her father's, a copy of an original that no one had seen. The friend had died, and perhaps to honor him they kept the me-

mento in the living room, even though they didn't like it.

"It's church stuff," they used to say.

In the lower right corner of the heavy frame, there was a small metal plate which read:

Island of the Dead

Renata loved the painting. She managed to have her piano placed so that during the long hours of practice she could easily look at it. She imagined herself within it: Death wouldn't scare her if it were to ferry her there. Renata felt as if she were already in that semi-darkness, amid sounds of winged feet, and sighs. Everything was vibrating, pulsating, in the scene's stillness. She could breathe the heavy air, touch the contours of the walls against the shadowy background. Tiny windows, cypresses, glassy black water. A boat was approaching, a shrouded figure was standing on its prow. The face, turned toward the Island, wasn't visible, but Renata imagined it to be emaciated, with phosphorescent eyes, the eyes of an animal in the dark. That being was concentrating on the task, watching over a coffin covered with a white cloth resting across the boat.

At the death of her parents, when she had sold the house in exchange for an apartment, Renata had taken the painting with her. A few years later, after she was married to Martin, who didn't like the painting, she had asked that it be moved to that house and hung at the landing, where the wooden stairs paused a bit before leading up to the darkness.

The painting was one of the souvenirs of Renata's earlier life, which had been a peaceful existence closed up in the large, well-lighted room of her music. She had been a solitary girl, a quiet adolescent, not sad, but isolated by discipline and solitude.

"No one has everything at the same time," her mother used to say. Renata played the piano when other girls played with dolls, she crossed the city, pale, clutching her music, when other young women went to the park with their boy-friends.

She had had only one boyfriend—her childhood friend Miguel, her guardian angel. Today it was difficult for her to picture his face. Perhaps he was married, perhaps dead.

Renata had loved him in her youth, in her own way, from a distance. She kept him in the background. Brief meet-ings, often postponed. She would sometimes forget about Mi-guel, needing to feel free to devote herself to her art, the force that dominated her from within.

He accepted everything without complaining. Miguel, the guardian angel, almost a brother. On her part, the love was simply an amusement, a diversion.

Renata's career began to come between them. Finally, when she started doing well, giving concerts, perfecting her art, the affection, the love, got in her way. Miguel meant a waste of precious time, and they decided that it would be best to break up.

He cried when they said good-bye. In order not to weaken, Renata had to be cruel. But at the last minute, she took his face in her hands and, kissing him, told him again, "I have nothing to give you, Miguel. Nothing. I have only one pas-sion in life, music." And she added with conviction, "I will never get married."

No, she hadn't lied. Only the piano could impose rhythm and order on the internal chaos that would over-come her if she stopped. Perhaps that's what art was, a bot-tomless compulsion, an endless effort of her soul to feel complete.

Later, married to someone else, Renata would often think of Miguel. Actually, her marriage meant betrayal not only of her calling but also of her old love. And when feeling lost she would remember Miguel and imagine how different everything would be if she had stayed with him. They had common roots and interests.

At first she hadn't missed him. But after her parents had died and a few years had passed, she grew lonely and she wondered whether she had made the right decision. Hadn't that uncompromising surrender to her career created an emptiness inside her now? She had been loved, but she had loved so little. She had been selfish. Perhaps it had been necessary, natural, to concentrate on her music. Yet slowly she was growing bitter.

"She has a gift," her family had said, when she had precociously shown talent for music, and they'd treated her as someone special, leading her to think innocently: I'm different from others. I am an artist.

It was both a privilege and a pain.

She had had neither time nor opportunity for deep friendships. All her relationships except that with Miguel were superficial. Pale and serious, but with the secret power she displayed at the piano, she may have intimidated young people her age.

When she met Martin she was restless and unhappy. Was that all there was to life? She had never made concessions to herself, she had never yielded to her body, which was demanding its rights too. How much time would she have for her own life, her own emotions, in addition to her interpretations at the piano of other people's joys and sorrows? And were the emotions she interpreted really those of others?

Alone in her apartment she began to lose interest in her books and records. Sometimes her art seemed a curse.

Renata turned her eyes away from her Island. Glancing down slightly she gazed at her dead son Camilo. For the first time she had to imagine him separated from his twin sister. Would he be complete in death without her?

Wouldn't he be afraid of the vigilant creature taking him to the Island on such a boat? Yet he seemed so peaceful during the crossing, looking like someone being caressed. We're never the same after someone . . .

He was always attracted to death, Renata thought.

Once at school a child had died, the son of some friends of the family and one of the few who had become close to Camilo. Carolina hadn't wanted to go to the wake, but Camilo had insisted, and Renata had had to take him. For over an hour he had remained seated next to the white casket, his little hands gripping the side, as he stared at what was left of someone who a few days before had been smiling at him.

On the way home he was so excited that he couldn't stop talking about what he had seen. But his mother noticed that he was talking to himself, recounting everything to himself, like someone describing the beauty of a painting in an exhibit. The dead boy's white face, his still shiny hair, his immobile hands.

"I touched them, but they were no longer his hands . . ."

Renata felt very sorry for him. The only real friend he had was now gone.

What she didn't know was that although he never again mentioned the boy's name, Camilo never forgot. A child like himself, perhaps nine or ten years old. The only person besides Carolina with whom he had been close. The first opening, the first possibility of contact outside the circle in which he and his other half had revolved since their birth.

For everyone else, the dead boy had been like any other child, though physically endowed with a beauty that neither Camilo nor his sister had. And Camilo loved beauty. He would cry when he heard it on his mother's piano, or when he saw it in the picture books around the house. He might even cry when, occasionally, light was reflected off someone's hair. Camilo loved too the delicate fairy-tale beauty of his young friend.

There was no intimacy between them. A mute adoration

in Camilo, with the other boy probably knowing nothing about it. But Camilo would inhale with pleasure the air his friend had breathed, he would rub his small thin hand on the other's clothes and afterwards when alone would hold his fingers to his face, thinking, these fingers have touched him.

In his lonely heart, Camilo had been in love. He hadn't understood it, nor had he measured his own individuality. But through that other child he had learned something, that there was a world outside himself and Carolina.

Then his friend had died. A brief illness and he was gone, he who but a few days before had been bending over a book with Camilo. At their side Carolina had sensed that Camilo inhaled only the air that came from his friend's nostrils.

After the death it was all over, and Renata relaxed. At that age children forgot quickly.

But the other boy was preserved. Without thinking often about him, Camilo knew: now he is mine forever. His beauty, his warmth, his love, all would mingle in a cloud, he thought, with a vague notion of possible happiness. In Camilo's memory, the face of the dead child dissolved, not even his scent remained, not even a gesture. All now belonged to that larger, more attractive realm. What is most beautiful is to be found in death, that I shall possess one day.

Renata couldn't have known of this that night. Perhaps even Camilo didn't know. Perhaps he hadn't seen in any other face a feature that could remind him of the dead boy he had once loved. Subtle are the webs of death.

Subtle: yet they had caught him, paralyzed him. Why hadn't he resisted? Why hadn't he tried to return to his mother, or to Carolina?

Early in the evening, Renata at times expected him suddenly to jump up and run around the room waving his arms and laughing his nervous laugh. He used to have such outbursts, which had worried her, mainly because he was usually so quiet.

Carolina never participated in them, she would smile in complicity at her brother, and watch him through her blond eyelashes. That's how the twins were, they had a somber pact. Or was it luminous? Renata could never tell. The children, so distant from her heart, whom she had loved with reticence and cold embraces, were nothing more to her than two graceful figures. Was the relationship touched by something sinister?

She thought about her daughter, asleep upstairs, the weaker half of the entity that was once Camilo and Carolina. Carolina had always followed her brother, adoring him, doing whatever he asked. Renata knew too that they communicated without words, their thoughts issuing from the same source, her womb and her heart.

They had been a single unit. Nothing outside themselves ever seemed to interest them much, engaged as they were in their fierce and silent struggle to be a unit.

But now Death had assaulted them. It had cut their circle down the middle. And no one knew what would become of Carolina.

"What will become of Carolina?" everyone asked, in a whisper in the living room, in hushed voices in the kitchen and in the garden. What will become of Carolina? The question floated in the air, in sighs, in moans. Even the inhabitant of the room upstairs at the end of the corridor may have noticed a change that night in the house, in the world, for her bell rang repeatedly.

The mother leaned forward to say "Son?" wanting to add "Where are you?" but holding back.

She addressed him hesitantly, as if without the right to speak to him like this. As if so solemn in his death he might arch an eyebrow, in that way of his, and gaze impenetrably at her.

Even if she did what Martin may have expected her to do, throwing herself on her son, kissing his hard and cold mouth, all night long, Camilo would feel nothing anymore. His mother's love, come too late, would not reach him. He was beginning to close himself off.

And she wanted to ask another question, the one everyone asks the dead: "What did I do for you, what did I give you?"

She had never spent so much time near him. There were details on his face that she had never before noticed. Even when her children were sick, she had had a nursemaid take over the bedside vigil, as she was nervous, grew tired easily, and needed peace.

But now there was time, that of a long night, and of the rest of her life, and thereafter.

Dead, would he be more accessible? Paradoxically, could he finally be his mother's son? What would he be like, alone, separated from his other half?

She had never really been his mother, she admitted, holding back a sea of bitterness welling up in her heart. But Camilo had never seemed to need her, because he looked to his sister, and the two were sufficient for each other.

Camilo and Carolina, a single fruit born split in two, dedicated to repair the rupture they had suffered. Perhaps that is why their bodies looked wasted, their eyes big with a pain they couldn't name.

The twins lived in a glass box, inaccessible to everybody outside. They had to be alike, they had to become one, they would accept nothing else. For Martin this obsession of theirs was crazy, a result of their mother's not disciplining them. But his anger accomplished nothing. Occasionally Camilo and Carolina pretended to obey, for a few hours, or even days. They read in separate corners of the house, slept in their own rooms, appeared to make friends with others. But everyone knew: This was only appearance, only temporary. The two of them were like dolls whose hair had been braided together, whose arms and legs and clothes had been tied together so that the slightest movement on the part of one would result in movement in the other.

They worked silently, laboriously, on a picture of themselves, creating with their blood and their thought their own image, the one they searched for, guessed at, gave birth to in anguish, the face and the name that would be theirs when they had finished.

It disturbed Renata to recall the efforts to separate the two. Different classrooms, once even different schools. Promises and punishments, Martin's screaming fits, meetings with psychologists and teachers, all for nothing. When they were apart, Camilo and Carolina would slowly lose their vitality, becoming empty, like the rind of a fruit whose juice had gone.

Finally, everyone except Martin had given up.

"That's the way they are," they said, as they had once said of Renata, "She has a gift."

Perhaps Martin was right when he blamed her for all of that. Could Renata have passed on to her children her own inner chaos? After abandoning her career, she felt she was coming apart, and was no longer whole. Where was her old self-confidence, her self-knowledge? She had grown sad. Her children had simply continued the search that she had had to relinquish.

Besides, she had never given them a mother's natural love. They were guests in her life, living beside her, and she was a guest in a daily routine in which she never felt at home. She forgave their idiosyncrasies, which she didn't always understand. She suffered knowing that at school their classmates singled them out for ridicule, but the twins didn't seem to care.

They enjoyed dressing alike to confuse people, with their identical tight pants and loose blouses, and their husky voices. They had fun deceiving their family and friends, switching places, until one day Martin discovered their tricks and laid down the law. From then on Camilo had to wear his hair short, and Carolina had to wear hers long.

Deep down, Renata admired them for their obsession. Not only were they not hurting anyone, they were easy to live with. Yet they weren't ordinary people, and Renata knew that this meant that they would be lonely.

But Martin could never have understood.

Obscured by the darkness, he rested his head on his hand. He was still an attractive man, although bitterness had left hard lines on his face.

Who could have thought that that stern mouth once uttered words of love while exploring Renata's body?

I threw myself into his arms to escape loneliness, and it was all deception, she thought. I was fleeing from myself. What I really wanted was to be alone, after getting married I discovered that I needed solitude. And Martin loved me too much. Can one love too much? Yes. He never left me alone. When he had to leave for work I knew that he had stayed with me in his thought, demanding things from me, caring for me, controlling me.

He was always asking: "Are you happy? Why this sad face? Why don't you enjoy anything? Why don't you like the farm? Why don't you help Clara in the kitchen?"

He would bend over me in bed at night, while I pretended to sleep, searching the face of the woman he loved, wondering: Where is she, what does she think about, whom does she dream of?

I didn't have enough room to be unhappy, Renata remembered. And every time I got depressed I felt guilty: Why am I doing this to Martin? Why can't I be a good wife?

At one point she began drinking. When she was alone, she would force the burning liquid down her throat, swallow enough to feel dizzy, then go to bed for a fitful, sticky sleep. Drunk, she would become even more miserable. After a few months she quit. She was already neurotic, would she be a drunk as well? That would be intolerable.

Then she intoxicated herself with music, and with solitude, when she could get it. Slowly she deteriorated. And yet she struggled with herself. I am coming apart, she concluded, I am disintegrating like something that falls into the water and gets soaked, heavy, limp. Repulsive.

II

Was it a girl? Or a boy? One couldn't determine the sex of the person on the bed, hair covering the face, hands pressing against the sex, between the thin legs. She was on her side, closed up like a pocket knife. An oyster. She was Carolina, but she could have been Camilo: the name would have fit her equally well. What was between her legs seemed unimportant. It merely said that she was Carolina, who wore her hair long.

The details of appearance served to placate other people. But the twins' reality lay on their inner stage, where they acted out the drama of their own truth, where they measured step by step the geography of their separation and analyzed the possibility of overcoming it. Everything else was unimportant to them. They ignored the audience of suspicious faces watching them.

Carolina awakened slowly. Someone had given her a shot earlier when she was crying hysterically, and she had slipped into the void from which she now emerged nauseated and cold.

20

They gave me a shot, she thought. She moaned, and turned over, drawing up her legs again, pressing against her aching sex. "Don't leave, Camilo!" she wailed.

She couldn't believe it, but neither did she have the courage to go downstairs to find out. Was Camilo really in a coffin in the middle of the living room? From the top of the stairs that afternoon she had seen him lying on the sofa by Mother, who was trying to support his hanging head. His forehead was covered with a bloody bandage that made his face seem even smaller.

Carolina saw horror in everyone's eyes. And all heads but Camilo's had turned to her as if to ask, What now?

Later she heard people say that he was dead. It was impossible, impossible! But hadn't she sensed all afternoon that something was wrong? Hadn't her body felt weighted down, weary, depleted, as if life were escaping her forever?

Camilo and she had always lived on limbo's narrow banks. If he traveled where she couldn't follow, she'd be lost.

But maybe it was one of his jokes. Despite everything, despite the horrified faces, it could be a joke. He was crazy about weird games. When little they often played like this, they played at dying, and Camilo was always the one to initiate it.

They would lie down on their two beds, stretch out, cross their hands on their chest, and close their eyes. At first Carolina would have to force herself not to laugh. But gradually she would get caught up in the game. By chance, sometimes, when really concentrating, they would feel transformed. A fog would cover them, a wave would try to swallow them, sucking them up, sucking them by their feet. They would grow pale, their breathing would become slow and slight, the great sleep would devour them, forever.

It was Carolina who would end the game. She'd get up, dizzy, and run towards her brother. And she would have to call him or touch him to get him to come back to reality, so absorbed would he get in the make-believe.

Then sometimes Camilo had fits. He would run around the room waving his arms, laughing madly, and then he would hug her and say, "I was just fooling! To scare you."

Carolina changed her position. As she lay on her back, she turned towards the ceiling the profile which had the same line as that of the wax mask exposed in the coffin in the living room. Her eyes, wide open, were identical to those the dead boy now hid behind his lids: large yellow eyes, almost the color of his hair.

What were Camilo's eyes looking at? What had they sought so eagerly in her eyes?

Lately he would quietly seat himself beside his sister, hold her hand, and gaze at her for a long time, much as they had done when they were children and were playing the staring game.

But it was not a game anymore. It was a search for something, a search at times agonizing, at times sweet, at times frightening. He probed deeper and deeper, with greater and greater persistence, and she had no answers for him. She returned his gaze as if she were an echo, only an echo. A word? What word?

Adolescents, they sometimes got no closer than this. The thoughts that circled them, that usually flowed between them so easily, more freely than their blood, were blocked.

No matter how much they resembled each other physically, they would occasionally discover, in one little thing or another, a barrier, and they suffered more and more each time they noticed this kind of imperfection.

He never loved anyone but me, thought Carolina.

(Or did he once love a boy now dead? She no longer remembered.)

She closed her eyes, withdrawing into herself, thinking: If Camilo is dead, I too have begun to die.

When they were born, they were not identical, though they resembled each other, like any two siblings of different sexes.

22

Both of them were small and weak. But with time they had become more and more alike. Without the courage to admit it, Renata knew, everyone knew, that they had *trained* themselves to be identical.

They practiced being identical with the same tenacity with which she had prepared herself for her piano in days gone by. And they acquired, one from the other, the same posture, the same manner of turning their heads, of holding a book, of walking. Their secret.

It enclosed them with a halo, and isolated them. People were curious at first, but then felt uncomfortable around them, not knowing if the two were playing. Were the twins secretly mocking them? Why did they seem to analyze everything with that air of superiority?

Renata had never seen such strange children or adolescents, except for herself when she had been confined to the piano. But she had had Miguel, and a close relationship with her parents. The twins didn't seem to love anyone.

Martin would get annoyed. "A boy who is always with his sister will turn into a queer."

And he had tried to separate them. When Camilo was little, he used to take him to the farm, to show him how charming farm life was, the kind of life that would be Camilo's. But Camilo refused to have fun, refused even to eat. Instead, he would cry and get sick. Martin would bring him back, and in a state of exasperation shove him through the door, and sometimes even hit him. Martin grew increasingly violent.

He was more tolerant with Carolina because he expected less from her. Her small stature, her pale complexion that neither medicine nor the sun from Mother's garden would cure, her peculiarities—none of it bothered her father. But the same characteristics in Camilo tormented him.

Mother always argued that they shouldn't force the children to do anything. As the twins got older they would improve physically and would become happier and more sociable.

Martin wouldn't give up. He didn't understand his strange son, who would never be his heir, who would never help him either in his business and on the farm. Camilo was as disturbing to him as was Renata. Since he had known her, Martin had not had the orderly, simple life he'd always liked. His hours of sleep, his hours of being awake, his thought, even his skin—everything was absorbed by the anxiety of loving Renata. And the seed of her womb had been affected as well: Camilo and Carolina, unexpected fruit, alienated from the world in which they had to grow up.

They had a gift, thought Renata, fighting to keep from crying again. And they developed it much better than I developed mine.

"What did I do with my gift?" she asked herself. How long has it been since I've played? More than six years? And did it change anybody's life?

She stretched her hands out flat, to look at her thin, strong fingers, now out of practice. They had lost their power to charm. Too much time away from the piano, when she was suppressing her desire to play, attempting to free herself of it. Often restless, she would get up at night and walk through the streets, or through the fields if they were at the farm. She had to have a release for her energy in order to feel whole again, if only precariously whole.

During the early years she often played the piano, every time she could be alone. She would send the twins to Mother's house and then play for herself, shivering with pleasure. And shivering with pain, as well, for she knew that in her failure to practice she had lost her agility. She belonged to another world now, and no longer had her old contacts or her audience. She would never be a great pianist.

And neither did her new life thrill her. Unprepared for

domestic responsibilities, she felt ill at ease and awkward. She was actually in charge of two households, for they also had the farm where they spent time and where Martin would bring his friends, whom she didn't like. She didn't understand them, or their vulgar, superficial wives who looked on her with suspicion.

Mother and Clara tried to befriend her, but even though the three got along well together, Renata couldn't understand them either. How could they spend so much time and energy on food, clothes, maids—the interests of those reconciled to a narrow-minded existence?

Martin saw what was happening but was unable to help. Renata was undergoing a transformation, as the beauty that once blossomed from within her died, and she became a worn out, slovenly woman with defeated eyes.

When she had no piano at hand, or when she went out with Martin, or when they had friends over, or when they were alone at home, she would sometimes become abstracted. With her eyes half closed, she would run her fingers across an imaginary keyboard and keep rhythm with slight movements of her head. If she was in the presence of others, who would be surprised by her behavior, Martin would get embarrassed.

Now I am reduced to playing a piano in the air, thought Renata. She drew up her knees, resting her elbows on them, caught in the memory of the times she had once played for real, of the last time she had played powerfully, the afternoon in which Angel Rafael . . .

She covered her face with her hands as tears ran through her fingers and dropped onto her skirt.

She wanted to get up, move around, see what Carolina was doing. But she stayed there, motionless, finding even breathing difficult.

What had she made of her life? What had she done to her husband? To her children?

The living room, the house, a pool of muddy water churned up by creatures of spit and shadows. Fear.

Where was the Island? Where were the dead? And what was that thing called Death? She had longed for it often as a liberation from her torment. If she were to die everyone would be happier, she felt. Martin, the twins, everyone. Anyway, for them my presence is already abstract, a melancholy shadow.

After some time she straightened up, wiped her face with her handkerchief, and began to look closely at Camilo. The expression on his face was still one of astonishment—the surprise of someone who receives a wet, intimate kiss of love on his mouth. He seemed to be saying: So this is what it is!

Every second he died a little more, as the Lover clung to him, covering his skin, devouring his heart. Camilo was immersing himself in waters where the concerns of the living were a wreckage from which he had to free himself.

All human relationships involve suffering. Yet if they had said this to Renata when she had met Martin and a few months later when she had married him, she would not have done anything differently.

Before her marriage, she had merely let herself be loved. To her, others meant tranquility so that she could play. She loved them because they cared for her and didn't bother her, she loved them almost as impersonally as she loved the faces of the public who admired her and trembled with emotion.

Art had made her self-centered, for it was the only love of her life. But wasn't that the way it had to be? She often asked herself: Didn't she have to be like this, giving all her passion to her art, to be a good pianist? Wasn't that always the price?

But upon meeting Martin she became preoccupied with the loneliness of her life and aware of her own sexuality, which she had been repressing.

No, she wouldn't have believed them if they had warned

her on the eve of her wedding. The ties of love can tear us apart, they are webs that can trap and strangle us. Just as a butterfly abandons its cocoon, she had thought that she could exchange her identity for that of Martin's wife.

To Miguel, her first boyfriend, she had said with a final kiss, "I have nothing to give you." But she had much to give Martin, a love whose intensity made the affection she had had for Miguel seem fraternal.

It was also useless for friends to say to Martin, "She is a fine young woman, she is even a great pianist, but she's not for you."

"Yes, yes," he would say, "she's different, and that's precisely why I'm going to marry her."

Experience had taught him that life is easy if we face things directly. A practical man, he fled from complicated, dangerous emotions.

He had been reared by Mother, a distant relative who had been a substitute for his own mother, who had died so early that he hardly remembered her, and he had two younger sisters: Clara, a blood sister, and Ella, Mother's daughter, whom Mother had brought with her when she came to care for them.

Later, Martin's father married her and died shortly thereafter. Mother took charge of the business and of their life, giving the children the sense of security they needed. Mother was their world.

At a young age Martin tended to the family's business affairs. He grew to prefer the farm to the city.

When he met Renata, he too was feeling lonely, wanting ties, a stable emotional relationship. He wanted a woman to sweeten his life and give him relief from his hard work.

(But she wasn't the one to do it.)

That night Martin didn't even recognize Mother's house, the house where he had lived as a child, where he had played,

27

where he had run up and down the stairs with Clara and Ella. Now, the smell of candles and flowers, the dragging hours, the death which he couldn't accept, which he couldn't understand. He felt like a child again, in his helplessness, and he angrily wiped away the uncontrollable tears. He avoided looking at the dead body. It unnerved him, so empty and so present, dominating everything.

Looking at Renata, he began thinking: We're getting old. What have we made of our lives?

All night long, their love, the promises, the hopes, the dreams, the intimacies, rolled from one corner to another of the room, evoking unwanted emotions.

It was Death that touched everything. Smiling, raising the ashes, putting a meatless finger here and there, rekindling the fire. And blood, live-red blood.

Death did not ask his permission.

Martin had met Renata almost by chance, at a concert he'd gone to with friends. He didn't appreciate the arts. In the spotlight on the stage, the pianist reminded him of a figure in a museum. He went to museums only if convenient. Angels playing lutes, that's what he had thought about when he saw her.

He had been impressed. She was delicate, and he was amazed when she unleashed on the piano energy he had never imagined, he felt moved to tears. Normally he would have resisted these emotions, which he judged unmanly, but in the darkness of the concert hall, he let himself go in pain and pleasure.

He asked to be introduced to the pianist, who up close appeared less striking. She wasn't particularly young, or pretty, and she was timid. She actually seemed unwell. But looking at her he couldn't forget the energy she had hidden within her, the power.

In person she seemed unapproachable, nice enough, but

with strange mannerisms. Her pale, yellow eyes, fascinating and unfathomable, belonged to their own entertaining world.

Renata was a challenge for him, and Martin wanted to make her soul his. He would possess even her art, and his friends would envy him for having such an unusual wife.

Soon he discovered in her an ardent, lonely body desperate for love. A few months later they were married.

But on this sticky night, all of that was lost, buried. Martin and Renata, buried too. They looked at each other cautiously, sending silent pleas for help, for an explanation, silently accusing each other. Even though she was getting old, Renata still disturbed him. What was that charm in her which had seduced him twenty years before, and which she still had? Seeing her onstage, he had said to himself: I must have her. The conquest had been easy, because however brilliant she was under the lights, however surrounded with admiration and affection, Renata was delicate, weak. So much in need of love that Martin had been profoundly stirred.

He wanted to make her happy, to be happy with her, in the simple, practical life that had always been his.

But Renata belonged to another world. And everything proved difficult for her. After she had first given herself passionately to Martin, in her thirst for love, she began to draw back. She seemed to find their life together disagreeable. She would get caught up in unexplainable depressions, and would become irritable and nervous. Could she be longing for the career she had interrupted at its peak? For Martin nothing could be better for a healthy life than a house, a family, and something useful to do. That was success, and that was what his wife needed.

Perhaps she missed her friends, whose letters made her unhappy for hours. And her crazy habit of locking herself in the living room and playing alone, with a passion she never expressed with him—wasn't she even then getting away from him little by little?

29

For the first time Martin felt disoriented by a woman, baffled. He couldn't reach her.

In those days they continued to attend concerts. He would watch her in the darkness. Seated at the edge of her seat, tense, concentrating, she seemed to return to a dimension where she could be herself, after which she would be fragmented once again.

Martin felt sorry for her, "She is suffering, very much, and I can't help her."

"I think that I was born without the natural instincts other women have," Renata had complained to her doctor after the twins were born. He reassured her that not all women were alike, that this would come with time, but his paternal smile had not calmed her. Even before pregnancy she had begun to think that the marriage had been a mistake. No matter how much she loved Martin, she ached to be with her music. That was her real life.

She thought that she could leave her career fairly easily. In the passion of the moment it seemed the natural thing to do—postpone it. Later, who knows, she might play again. There was even a piano at the farm house. And her own piano, the one that had been in her apartment for many years, she could take to her new home . . . Everything would be OK.

But she learned differently. The yearning for her career, her boredom with a domestic life and her lack of aptitude for it, all interfered in her relationship with Martin, who wanted an energetic and capable wife, a woman like Mother.

She felt offended, angry. I'm an artist, she thought. What am I doing here with these people, with their problems and their petty concerns?

Even making love she could no longer please him. And Martin would demand that she be uncomplicated like an animal.

"But I am not an animal!" she would answer, trying to smile and feeling humiliated.

Later, thinking that she didn't love her children as much as she should, Renata decided that her previous life, focused entirely on her music, had now made it impossible for her to be unselfish. Unless she were suffering from some biological deficiency. Could that be possible?

As if in protest of the joyless union that had brought them into the world, Camilo and Carolina, frail as babies, were not developing properly. A real disappointment for Martin—they were not by a long shot the healthy children he had wanted.

During the difficult pregnancy, Renata nourished only one hope, that she could be free of it, that she could get rid of it. To do so would be wrong, damnable, she knew, but she was different from other women. She wasn't happily anticipating the birth, she was afraid.

After the Caesarian she awoke depressed. What was she to do now? How was she to care for such weak, premature babies? How could she pretend to be happy when what she felt was fear, anguish, and only an ambiguous affection for them?

They hired a nursemaid. But she was tormented by the question of whether it was right to entrust her children to a complete stranger. Shouldn't she carry out her responsibilities herself, even if she did feel incapable of it? She couldn't relax when she was with the twins, not until she was out of their presence.

She often got hysterical, and she fought with Martin, who was just as impatient and unhappy as she. With her grating, metallic voice she questioned him and scolded him, for she felt betrayed. He had made her abandon her real life, had seduced her with his strength and his passion, had taken advantage of her loneliness, and now was binding her to a life that seemed purposeless, that held no attraction for her whatsoever.

"You don't even nurse your children!" Martin had yelled at her once in a heated argument. The accusation was true: the painful and tiring act disgusted her. She couldn't explain it. With the two mouths sucking at her, taking from her juices she could never get back, she felt she would never be whole again.

The doctor had told her that depressions were common in women after childbirth. Although he was not eager to do so, within a month he had her stop the breastfeeding.

The marriage had been a mistake. Without strength to make further changes in her life, Renata slowly began to waste away, just like the invalid in the closed room, in Mother's house.

III

The dead boy lay between them like an extermi-
nating angel, imposing silence, implanting separation, cutting
last ties, and weaving other ties, of bitterness and pain. Not
even over the corpse of their son were they together again—
the love which might have helped them was insufficient.

Avoiding Martin's eye, Renata got up, rubbed her hands
to warm them, and went over to stand by the casket. The
stench of decomposing flesh already issued from Camilo's
body. Why wasn't death cleaner? Without agonizing smells,
with the subtle scent of perfume, the scent Camilo used to
have?

Renata bent forward and sniffed the flowers, without revealing that she was detecting through their fragrance the
odor which she feared others might notice.

Wasn't that stench still there, in spite of the efforts she
and Mother had made that afternoon, that smell that
Camilo had had when they had laid him on the sofa?

With a handkerchief she wiped away the moisture that continued to sully his brow like a breath, a sweet blow. Who was embracing him now, who was to love him? So far as Renata knew, he had never loved a woman. Not a single girlfriend, not anyone intimately. Only Carolina, always Carolina.

If he had grown up, would he have felt other pulls, other desires?

Still bending over, peering at him more closely, she drew back her hand suddenly and clasped it to her mouth to suppress a cry. The dead boy's face had changed.

The initial air of astonishment had brightened into a smile. Camilo was almost smiling in the wrinkles around his eyes, at the corners of his mouth. Not a smile of irony, or of superiority, with which the dead sometimes say good-bye, but a timid, charming, childish smile.

Could it be the effect of the candlelight, or of her own exhaustion? No, it was there, the dead boy was changing with the passage of time. Cold, still: a statue lying on the tomb of an ancient prince. Such a delicate face, such slender hands, all of him pure absence, stone. Far away from ordinary life, as he had always been. Camilo studied, ate, walked, and talked, but he was not like other people. He and Carolina—guests, visitors, waiting for the moment to go back. To where?

She didn't know. The dead boy's smile indeed was there. He wanted to say something. But he wouldn't say where he was, he couldn't. What was the message? What was his message? What was his new language?

Perhaps relief, perhaps liberation, his mother thought.

He has now found what he so desperately sought in his relationship with Carolina. He wanted an explanation, and all he could discover was his own face duplicated in that of his sister. Now he is on the other side.

He moved toward death like someone who has finally

found his way. The boat, where was his boat? Who was guiding him? Who would serve as his mother, sister, lover, friend, or father?

Renata glanced quickly at the painting on the landing of the stairs. She loved it more than ever, part of her life was already there.

Camilo was performing for the first time on the stage of his death, by the candles' weak light, with the smile of someone who does not yet know his lines but is going to do his best.

Martin extinguished his cigarette in the ashtray, spreading the ashes around in the metal bowl. He wanted to make Death retreat, or else to demand, in the house, in the city, that the slow and painful ritual, which he could not control, be expedited. In fact, he felt his son's death, under the circumstances, to be his own failure, he felt shame, humiliation.

What had he made of his marriage? Frustration, separation, those weird children, and now . . . this.

That night Martin felt nonexistent. Emotional conflicts always left him feeling tense, strained, but death was worse—it left him devastated. He didn't know how to act. Everybody hugged him murmuring the same thing: He was so young . . . what a tragedy. . . . They pretended not to know that Camilo had killed himself. They'd say behind Martin's back, "He killed himself because of his father . . ."

Martin forced himself not to think about this. He tried to remember things that might cheer him up—life in the country, friends, work. He did not permit himself to think of women now, but he had had many, especially right after they had separated. In recent years, however, every new affair left him emptier inside. He felt ridiculous, old.

He stretched out his legs, keeping his hands in his pockets even while remaining seated.

He still could not believe it, his son was dead. He hadn't

even had an opportunity to get to know him. The delicate boy, the effeminate adolescent, had made him impatient, angry, afraid. Now he was almost transparent, defenseless, exposed. But out of reach. Time had been lost on that disturbed life, and there was no way to recuperate it.

Martin shut his eyes tight, cleared his throat, clenched his fists inside his pockets. Camilo had been stronger than he after all. He had not given up until the end, and he had won a space for himself where no one could bother him. He was free.

Renata. What might she be feeling? Maternal love, that so belatedly might be tearing her apart? Remorse? What about her relation to him? During that night of confrontations, what might she be thinking of her ex-husband? Was she perhaps lamenting their failure? Could she be feeling, as he felt, that everything had been deception, or did she retain some bright moments in her memory? Moments of love did not belong in the solemn presence of Death. Or did they?

What he should have done was to run away from her. Renata had passed on to her children her inability to adapt to the world. These two ghosts came from her soul.

Even during that tragic evening, she was not reacting to things the way a normal woman would. She hardly cried, and she spent the entire time looking at that damned picture that he should have had removed. Or worse—he knew that Renata was playing her piano in her mind, an irritating habit that had always disconcerted him.

Martin got up and walked to the other side of the room, taking great strides, ignoring the faces turned towards him, profaning the silence the occasion demanded.

He felt alive. He leaned against the wall, so that he could see his wife.

Renata had never been pretty, now she was ugly. Her profile, which years ago he had considered delicate, was nothing more than a long nose and a receding chin, her curly hair was pinned back severely. Yet even like this some-

36

thing in her still disturbed him. Martin fought the emotion. Could he be feeling at the same time both anger and love?

Once he had confessed to friends that he had married an iceberg with a bright, glistening surface, whose truth was submerged in a frozen, dark green sea.

Often when they were newlyweds, late at night, he had heard her get up out of bed, lock herself in the living room, and play the piano. In this act there was a passion, a despair, that seemed abnormal to him. He listened in an effort to understand her, to excuse her, for he wanted to recapture the woman whom he thought he had married. What was missing in her life? How had he disappointed her? Tears of loneliness and impotence would run down his face. He had been betrayed. Betrayed and humiliated, because he suspected that even when making love, passive and tense, with her hands stretched out on the sheet beside his body, she would move her fingers as if stroking the keys.

Martin began to walk around again. The floorboards creaked, he was fat and tired. He had worn himself out administering and expanding his property, for nothing. Even Camilo, in whom he had had some hope, briefly, at first, had ended up hating the farm, and perhaps even his father.

Martin felt a choking sob rise up in his throat, his eyes watered. He wanted to get out of there, to be smothered by the fog, to disappear.

But he returned to his chair and began the vigil again. His hands shook with his effort to keep himself under control. Or was it that he was trying to keep from reaching out to caress the drooping shoulders of the woman he had loved?

He had barely sat down when the buzz of the bell gave him a start, and he was embarrassed. Wasn't everybody in the household accustomed to those calls by now? They seemed to come from a soul in torment.

A cry for help. Even so, nobody, except for Mother, ever

37

answered. Nobody would bat an eye, they would all keep on doing whatever they were doing—Clara dusting the old furniture, the twins reading some book together, Renata absorbed in something, or, other times, playing silently in the music room. It was as if the sick person didn't exist, or as if everyone were deaf, blind.

But that night Martin trembled at the buzzing of the giant insect who dominated the house. He felt sorry for Mother. He imagined her stumbling out of bed, adjusting her wig on her head—they hadn't seen her without it for many years—and going down the hall.

She did everything without complaining, maintaining her good humor and vitality even after she had grown old.

Martin smiled thinking about her—her blond wig, her excessive makeup, her unfashionable clothes.

In his imagination, he accompanied her to the door of the room. He lit a cigarette, took a puff, inhaled deeply. He didn't want to think about it, having banished to a corner of his consciousness the creature that suffered an inhuman destiny behind the door whose key Mother was turning now.

He tried to keep the image away, but it overtook everything. A girl with black hair and sensual mouth, a beautiful mouth. A beautiful woman full of the juices of life, whom he had loved and who had loved him too, in the splendor of their youth.

Ella. Who would have chosen for the fatherless girl a name so ambiguous, so prophetic, of half humanity and half absence?

Love had been forbidden, because for Mother, for relatives and friends, the two were siblings. Reared together from the time they were little, it was as if they had been born from the same womb. Ever since they could remember they had been together.

And when in adolescence they became more passionately attracted to each other, Mother discovered them, and her stern disapproval had made them question whether their love was normal, allowable. Incest. The word weighed heavy on them. They didn't want to hurt Mother, that is, Martin didn't want to. He felt indebted to her, and his strong will, combined with the urgent messages of his heart and his body, conflicted with what he felt he was supposed to do.

The situation had dragged on for two, three years. Separations, attempts to forget, tumultuous, ardent meetings in secret on the farm or in some room in Mother's house. Agony and ecstasy at the same time.

But Mother had once more surprised them in each other's arms, and they had had a very serious discussion. Mother ordered Martin to spend one month away from the farm, where she and her daughter were spending their vacation. That was to give her time to arrange for Ella to live with some distant relatives.

But they had telephoned each other. Ella in tears, Martin in shock. Finally, they planned a secret meeting in the orchard behind the house, where she went regularly to pick fruit. Martin would come in from the city, he wanted to take her with him.

Ella had been sitting on the fence waiting for him. Perhaps, because of being in love and being excited, she had arrived too early, or perhaps Martin had been delayed. Anyway, fate had arrived on time, knocking the girl off the fence. A short fall, but catastrophic. Martin didn't see her again until a few days later, when she lay paralyzed in bed, hardly able to recognize him. Ella began a one-way journey away from him, to somewhere beyond. He could contemplate her from this side only.

With age and the long illness of her daughter, Mother became a symbol of dedication. Everyone called her Mother, even friends, servants, grandchildren. It didn't matter that the determined, lively woman had become a pathetic little old lady. She was the center of everyone's life: If ever I need her, Mother will be there.

Until she got married, Renata knew very little about her new family. Martin spoke often about Mother, and it was only much later that Renata found out that she was not even his real mother, she had taken the place of the one who had died when he was small. There was Clara, the younger sister—pretty, never married, who suffered from nerves because of some unhappy love affair she had had when young.

And later Renata had discovered that there was a third, a half-sister, Ella, who was very ill.

Renata became intrigued, for Martin's eyes would cloud over when speaking of her. Her strange name, his reticence aroused a curiosity in her.

"And this sister of yours never comes out of her room?"

Martin answered as if wanting to drop the subject. At first they had taken her out to get some sun, but as time passed she gained too much weight, and it was difficult to carry her. Besides, she was not conscious of much. It was hard on Mother, so at home, in order not to upset her further, no one mentioned the subject.

Martin had sometimes said, laughing, that Mother was a "crazy little old lady," but everyone adored her.

Nevertheless, Renata could not have pictured the figure that was waiting for her at the door of the house. An old woman, short, fat, with a wig of bouncy blond curls. False eyelashes, painted mouth, powdered, wrinkled cheeks. A yellow dress that was too big.

This character had greeted her in an unusually beautiful voice, "Well, aren't you going to embrace your old Mother?" Renata had been won over.

Clara, the sister-in-law, intimidated her a little. Tall, serious, almost imposing, with a beautiful face, heavily made up. A doll's face. Renata thought that she was ready to go to a party, with that elegant dress. Later she noticed that Clara was always like this. She would stay in her room for days, and then all of a sudden start stirring around, spend hours in a ritual of fixing herself up to look beautiful, and go down, watch television, leaf through magazines, talk a little, return to her room upstairs, and remove her makeup and clothes, without even having had a visitor.

Martin used to say that her nerves were shot. Perhaps she stared too fixedly, too darkly, perhaps she spoke in too much a monotone. She was cordial but reserved, she had some invisible wrap over her, like glass or varnish, which kept her from trembling.

Apparently she passed her time doing nothing. She went through phases of buying things, and she would go out every day to get clothes and accessories which she would display with the happiness of a child. She worked in the kitchen.

Other times there were dark periods. Few female friends. Occasionally some male friend of Martin's would ask her to go out, and occasionally she would accept.

Before long Renata began to feel that there was something strange about that house, there was that invalid in the closed room upstairs. Living in an apartment not far away, Martin and Renata would visit Mother almost daily. Daily, Ella worried them, weighed heavily on them, closed off as she was in her illness, and in the silence with which they tried to protect her.

Martin had warned Renata not to try to find out, not to torment Clara or Mother with her desire to see the invalid. Better to forget. Renata couldn't. There weren't even any pictures of Ella in the house, not a single photograph from the time when she was healthy, nothing. A living absence, an open wound.

But Renata had decided that given the opportunity she would ask to see the room.

She became even more curious when she discovered that Martin visited it fairly regularly, at least once a week.

One day she asked him, "What do you do in there?"

"I speak to her."

"But didn't you say that she doesn't know anything?"

"I keep her company for a while. You can't tell."

Seeing that he was suffering again, she decided not to insist.

She could not imagine that during his visits Martin talked with this non-existent being. It would be like talking in front of a tomb. He would sit down in the chair near the window, away from the bed, which was in the middle of the room, a hospital bed with a crank.

He tried not to look at what remained under the covers, not even to smell what was there. And he often spoke to her, at times just a few sentences. Other times, long monologues in which the real listener was the person who was both already dead and still alive. Alive not in that shapeless body, but in Martin's heart.

He talked about his business, about his friends, about his success. At first he didn't talk about Renata, but when everything began to fall apart, he opened up and told his lover, whom his memory still preserved beautiful and sensual. The Ella of the past, still perfect, waited for them to live together in love. Martin then talked about his failures and about his loneliness living with Renata, about his strange children, about his disappointments. It was as if she could hear him, hold his face against her warm breasts tightly, and console him.

Yes, she lived on, locked in the body that fought to breathe, with beady black eyes fixed on the ceiling, suffering unbearable pain.

Please don't let her know anything, implored Martin secretly. If she were able to think it would be too terrible.

What would Ella think about? What was in that heart of hers that to the doctors' dismay cruelly refused to stop?

Martin would talk and talk, he felt he could in this way fulfill a painful pact with a painful lover.

Mother welcomed Renata warmly. Her sagging bosom was a shelter for Renata and her problems and for her future children. It had ample room for everyone's sorrows and fears.

Mother had been worried because Martin did not get married right away. She feared that he was obeying some absurd fidelity to his lost love and did not feel free.

Years before, Martin and Ella, reared as siblings, had had an illicit love affair. Mother considered it illicit, forbidding its continuance because she found it shameful. Ella had been born before Mother had married, in a period in her life when she behaved poorly and suffered. That may be why Mother always treated her more coldly than she did her two borrowed children, Clara and Martin.

Mother had never before thought much about the fact that although they had been together from the time they were children there was no blood bond between them. She eventually discovered that Martin and Ella were meeting secretly. People had seen them embracing in the woods, someone had surprised them locked in her room.

Mother would not be diverted from her steadfast position. She blamed herself a little, for having permitted them too much freedom, after all she had considered them brother and sister. But she set things in order. She was a strong woman, who had taken charge of her family and her property and had put great effort and energy into managing it all.

Anyway, after Ella had had her accident and had begun to enter her subhuman condition, closing herself off from them, Mother often doubted herself: Had she done what she should have done? Destiny had relieved her of decision by taking Ella to that island. Yet at the same time it had insidiously roped Mother to a track. She could not leave the invalid, who insisted on her presence. Ella would allow only Mother to feed her, bathe her, care for her. At first, when she was more aware of things, she refused to receive visitors other than Mother and Martin. Clara looked in on her seldom, for her nerves got bad whenever she entered the room.

But afterwards, when she had submerged herself in that swamp and could no longer speak, the invalid continued to react to any strange presence, as if she could still smell, hear, perceive things with her skin. She wanted her mother, and would hold onto Mother tightly like an octopus sucking through thousands of tentacles. She now demanded and collected the love and understanding that she had rarely received when healthy and beautiful.

Perhaps because of remorse for having forbidden their love, and remembering Martin's violent reaction, Mother wanted very much for him to get married. But when she saw Renata she became frustrated, for Renata was not the woman for him. That distracted little bird might someday become a great pianist, but she couldn't accompany Martin in his rhythm.

Yet they were in love, and it was better for Martin to marry her than continue to hold on to the ghost of someone who no longer existed.

Renata became a part of the family, and without anyone telling her, she understood that she was not to ask about Ella, and that she, like everyone else in the household, was to say to any stranger asking about the invalid, "She is the same as usual."

Renata had also been frightened by the bell. She too had imagined Mother running to answer it, as she always did, without ever complaining, without ever losing her sense of humor. Mother was the mother of nobody, because the creature in the room had long since broken those ties. To be the mother of Ella was to be the mother of nothing.

I could never love anyone the way Mother loves this daughter, thought Renata, shifting her position in her chair. She contemplated her Island in order not to see, not even in her memory, what Mother might be facing upstairs. She preferred to focus on the painting, on its majestic and somber beauty. The pilot cloaked in white, standing in the prow of the boat, transporting Camilo toward nowhere.

But her memory of Ella persisted. That round, bright rock looked like the lifeless cheeks with which the invalid pressed the bell stuck to the pillow with adhesive tape. They had taught her to do it. Like a trained dog, poor Ella would turn her head and call . . . A ship in the night, emitting signals. Did she really want, as they assumed, merely to be relieved of hunger, filth, cold? Or was she lucid, and did she need to come out of herself, to escape the body to which she had been bound for many years. Inside that repulsive prison, could there still be a human being thinking, a human soul throbbing, desiring the salvation of love?

It would be terrible if she knew of her own condition.

Renata closed her eyes again: I have never loved anyone the way Mother loves this daughter. Mother, who had never nursed Clara or Martin, but who had been more of a mother to them than had she, Renata, to her own children.

Martin used to tell her that when they were small he and his sister were Mother's favorites, that she had rejected her real daughter.

But Ella collected what was due her. At home they all knew it. Now she complained day and night, she asked, she demanded, she imposed. Her overwhelming presence excreted subhuman signals, lamentations, orders. Sighs, moans, cries. Love me, care for me, look at me, like me! And

45

while the others pretended not to hear her, Mother would drop whatever she might be doing to go upstairs. And everyone would start thinking: Mother has a greatness that is touching.

Almost midnight.

The outside door had been closed to keep out the fog. At dawn there would be other visitors filling the house with their fear and their curiosity, asking: And the dead boy, how is the dead boy?

Mother and Clara were asleep. The invalid had not called again. Carolina too was probably resting. Having taken the tranquilizer, it would be best for her to sleep until morning. The day would be very difficult for all of them.

Renata looked at Camilo: Where would he be now? Dead, he seemed to her to be a little less mysterious. Perhaps less enigmatic now that the sphinx had swallowed all of the enigmas, the waters dissolving everything.

Camilo held up his yellow profile as if he were looking inward.

Why was I always so suspicious of them? she asked herself regretfully. It was absurd, but she had always been suspicious of her children. In their silences, in their little signals, in their smiles, she had imagined dark plots. Did they know disturbing secrets? What happened that day with Angel Rafael?

(And during their visits to the room at the end of the corridor?)

Sometimes she had asked Martin for help, but he would only criticize her when she presented him with a problem concerning the children.

"Did you know that the children have visited . . . the room?" she asked one morning, after wrestling several days with the decision of whether to tell Martin or to hide the fact from him?

46

He had put his cup down angrily, asking, "How do you know?"

"Mother's new maid told me."

"Does Mother's new maid spy on our children?"

"But the children . . ."

"They are not so little anymore. That's your crazy notion. In fact, they are almost ten, and they still sleep in the same room! If they went to visit Ella, they must have had a natural curiosity. And," he added hurriedly, "if they go in there, they won't want to go back . . ."

Renata had given up, fearing another argument. Practically all their discussions ended disagreeably those days.

Perhaps the maid really had exaggerated. She was new in the house, and had probably had her imagination excited by the closed room, and by the mysterious invalid.

"Are you sure . . . ?" Renata had asked.

"Yes I am. I went to look because I knew that nobody is supposed to enter there . . ."

"And what did you see in there?"

The girl, upset, twisted her apron between her hands.

"They . . . they mistreat her, ma'am."

"But, how do they mistreat her? That doesn't make sense!"

"They stab her with little scissors . . . they say bad words . . ."

Renata had felt such a chill that her teeth had chattered, and the little hairs on her arms had stood up on end. She asked the girl not to tell anyone, and a little while afterwards she succeeded in having Mother fire her.

For many days she felt torn between the desire to question the children and the fear of their reaction. Was that a malicious gleam in their yellow eyes?

It would be more comfortable to forget about it, or to pretend to forget. But she had not forgotten. When she looked at her twins she would start imagining what they might be doing in there. What in their souls draws them into that room? How do they get in if Mother has the key?

With horror she remembered her only visit to Ella, during the first months of her marriage. In spite of Martin's asking her to ignore the invalid, she spoke of her to Mother one day.

"May I go to her room with you?"

Mother showed surprise as she looked at her, but had nodded affirmatively.

Renata had entered the room behind her, becoming queasy from the smell, frightened by the darkness. Odors like those at the farm, to which at that time she was still trying to grow accustomed. Urine, feces, disinfectant. And another odor that only later was she able to identify, which emanated from the tremendous suffering.

She had expected to find a woman rendered noble by her illness, but she saw a creature lying on the bed who was hardly human.

A huge being, very fat, a large head, thin black hair, eyes fixed on the ceiling. How could Mother, who was now beginning to age, take care of that huge body all alone?

Renata had leaned against the wall, quickly trying to imagine something to say, but she had no voice.

Mother cranked the bed, stroked her daughter's head, and chattered on without stopping, as was her habit. When she was in distress, she made small talk without much sense. It distracted her.

"She was a good daughter," she said, busy with dresser drawers and linens. "She never gave me any trouble. She didn't even have a boyfriend, imagine that, and, mind you, she was quite a young lady. She played with Martin, she cared for Clara, as if they really were siblings. And when she was almost twenty years old, she fell off a fence there at the farm, such a silly thing. She fell awkwardly, and broke her back. She also must have injured her head, because after some time I noticed that she was not getting better, she had

48

almost stopped speaking. Now I believe that she doesn't know what is happening."

Mother opened a bottle of alcohol, whose pungent aroma concealed Ella's smell for a few minutes. Renata felt like saying that it was a good thing she didn't know what was happening.

She then moved away from the wall to approach the bed. Should she offer to help? The invalid was now turning her head from one side to the other, her eyes glazed over. Renata saw the bell attached to the pillow, the instrument of torture for Mother.

Ella had let out a strong blast of air. Mother turned down the sheets. Renata retreated a couple of steps, she didn't want to see, but she looked anyway, from a distance. Mother, leaning over the bed, impatiently adjusted her wig, which had become twisted around, and said in a normal voice, "Her period has started again."

Sheer horror expelled Renata from the Cave.

Second Part: The Waters

Death wears purple. With a
gold lamé rose in her wig—oh,
Death with her gilded rose,
smiling with arms crossed.
    LYGIA FAGUNDES TELLES

IV

The infinite hours of a wake at night.

Thinking about Ella, Renata remembered the smell of her dead son when he had been delivered to her that afternoon. Camilo, always well groomed, who was almost feminine in the way he took care of himself, who used his sister's cologne, who was repulsed by anything vulgar. He detested even the smells of the farm, complaining the whole time whenever they were there. But those smells clung to him, under the casket's flowers, reminding Renata of her husband's body when, their conjugal life already difficult, he still went to bed with her. The torment of intimacy.

At first, she had loved Martin uninhibitedly, to her slight embarrassment. Little by little, seeing that the distance between them was unbridgeable, and feeling guilty, she began to change. She hated herself whenever she experienced pleasure with him. And she wanted to punish herself for the physical bliss that made her body desire his so fervently while her soul suffered its solitude.

She grew bitter. She hurt Martin consciously, tormented him, argued. During the increasingly rare reconciliations, he would take her in his arms and let her cry on his chest, holding her without understanding her, he too suffering.

"What is the matter with you? What do you need?"

She couldn't answer, because she couldn't see a way out, she couldn't return to the life she had led before. Her interrupted career, her long absence from the stage, her lack of practice, her feeling of helplessness, all made such a return impossible.

They hurt each other, and they drew apart, unavoidably.

They quarreled even in front of the children. Camilo and Carolina listened to their arguments silently and solemnly, clinging protectively to each other in a corner of the room.

Our life was sheer destruction, Martin thought, his face hidden in shadow. The relationship disintegrating, Renata transformed, problems with the children, himself busy, troubled, caught up in the demands of his work, every day understanding less what was happening. At home his wife was withdrawn and hostile. He often felt compassion for her, realizing that the marriage had been a mistake. In her effort to move into his universe, Renata had come apart inside, and his love was not sufficient to keep her whole.

"I was born this way," she would sometimes say, holding him tight.

Not even motherhood had resolved the situation. Instead, it gave Renata a sense of disintegration in her production of two more parts of herself. She was drowning in the gap between what she had been and what she was no longer able to be.

Martin pressed his fingers against his aching head.

He closed his eyes for a long time, and when he opened them he received such a shock that he almost screamed. Dead Camilo was standing on the landing. Then he saw that it was Carolina, with her hair tied back. She took a step forward, staggered, and grabbed the frame of the painting, leaving it crooked.

Martin started to leave his chair, wanting to run over to help her, but stopped and sat down again. He had never been very affectionate with his children, now he didn't know how to begin. Besides, he feared that Carolina would create a scene, which he would hate to have happen. It would be embarrassing, and frightening. He, who had thought himself so strong, felt his heart about to explode. The whole living room, the whole house, was a soap bubble ready to burst, turning so quickly that it seemed to stay still. At the slightest touch, everything would dissolve.

Martin glanced at Renata, her face delicate and pale, as if she were dead, her eyes big, her mouth carelessly open.

Carolina regained her balance by herself. She came down the stairs without looking at anyone. She paused in front of her brother.

"Where are you?" she called aloud, in the husky voice of an old woman.

She was panting like Ella, when Ella would roll over and over in the solitude of her room in her private game.

No one moved. The drowsy visitors were watching her, once again interested. One of them got up to see better.

Renata figured that she had to do something—speak to her daughter, get her out of there. But the fatigue and the pain enfolded her like wet rags, making it impossible for her to react to what was happening. And there was not the love or intimacy between them that might have allowed her to say or do something to her daughter now.

I was never her mother either, she thought, staring at her daughter's narrow shoulders, her devastated face. She pitied her. What would Carolina do now, without her other half, the stronger half, the bolder half? Camilo had always taken charge, Carolina had always followed him, with a look of veneration.

Suddenly the young woman was flat on the floor. She had slid slowly to the floor, bumping the metal structure which held the casket and rocking it dangerously. Martin jumped up, choking back a cry, but the casket and its wax passenger settled down once more. Curled up on the ground, practically under Camilo, Carolina turned into an animal, twisting into a position to die.

Martin leaned down to give her his hand, but then noticed her eyes, glittering, fierce, through the hair that partially hid her face. He quickly drew back, hearing from her a horrible sound, a growl. She's going to bite me, he suddenly realized.

A growl that made Renata's flesh creep, her heart pound, her throat tighten up.

She forced herself to intervene, almost unable to speak. "Daughter . . . don't do that . . ."

But she too was afraid to touch her. In her suffering Carolina was beyond her reach. Flat on the floor, with her ear pressed to the ground, she seemed to be listening to the steps of a dance, solemn, slow—Camilo's steps, as he danced round and round with Death, further and further away from them.

Perhaps Mother had been waiting, listening, attending with her heart, the way she always did. Never angry, she could predict the buzz of the bell.

She was descending the stairs, wearing her old robe over

56

her nightgown. She had put on her wig, and she still wore her false eyelashes, even though she must have already been asleep.

With her belly protruding, she waddled in. She bent over her granddaughter, who was not of her own flesh and blood, and spoke to her in a low voice. Then she touched her on her shoulder.

Carolina slowly untwisted herself, got up, and stood by Camilo. Bending over the casket, she contemplated him for a long time, hugging herself as if for protection. She did not speak. In the living room all stared at her silently, including Renata and Martin.

Still looking at no one, as if nothing existed except herself and the dead boy, Carolina left the room on the arm of the old lady.

A great dignity emanated from them. Mother was leading away a person condemned to death who had already begun to die. As a survivor, she would become a little contaminated by the decay. Carolina's arms and legs, body, soul would slowly die, and there was nothing anyone could do.

The two went up the steps together. They did not stop at the landing where the Island was hanging at an angle.

A bizarre fat old lady, a thin adolescent looking ill. On their heels, a throat's blast of air, repugnant, pursuing them from behind and awaiting them at the road's end.

Someday, we shall all go there, they thought. Everybody. And each gave in to the contemplation of destiny, aware that the end, where Mother had arrived, and the beginning, where Carolina was now, were connected by the same mechanical spring, winding up and winding down. The waters of a thousand shipwrecks.

Perhaps because she had watched Mother's blond wig disappear up the stairway, Renata suddenly had a vision of Angel Rafael, and she hid her face in her hands. She didn't want it, she didn't want it. She didn't even know for which of her children she would weep now.

Angel Rafael was mentioned almost as infrequently as Ella in Mother's house. And since he could not buzz any bells or send any signals from where he was now, his existence was even more ambiguous than that of the invalid. But both infiltrated the world with their presence.

He had been born when Camilo and Carolina were almost ten years old. A late pregnancy. His parents were already openly discussing a separation. Actually, Martin was almost never home, he spent a lot of time at the farm, and in the city he slept in his office.

But Renata had become pregnant during one of their brief reunions, intense, painful encounters that ended in bitter arguments. She had thought about an abortion but lacked the courage, and in the end had an easy pregnancy.

Martin had treated her with kindness, and she had made an effort to reciprocate. Mother and Clara frantically made clothes, arranged things for the baby. Renata gave birth normally to a beautiful boy, and then holding him in her arms forgot her labor pains.

His parents loved him with a boundless, suffocating love. And they loved him for the possibility of repairing their lives as well.

All at once Renata felt like a mother. That late-born child was hers who awakened waves of warmth in her womb, in her heart.

Martin even changed his hours of work and his trips to the farm in order to play with him. Clara and Mother argued over the pleasure of holding him on their laps. Only the twins ignored him. From the day he was born, when someone would ask them whether they liked their little brother, they would answer in unison, very seriously, "I don't know."

58

The baby grew. He was healthy, quiet, content, free of the problems that had plagued his siblings.

Because he was so happy, and blond, everyone called him Angel Rafael.

Renata didn't want that memory to push into her mind tonight, she fought the memory and the grief. During those six years she had trained herself to do so the way she had once trained her fingers, wrists, body, and mind to play. Don't think, don't remember, don't feel, she had commanded herself.

But when Angel Rafael kept returning, she would go crazy and leave the apartment, walk through the night, in the rain, in the cold, shaking in her suffering. Not even at the piano could she find relief, her fingers were never again to touch a keyboard.

Could he too be on the Island? she had asked herself looking at the painting. It was difficult to imagine him there, in that lugubrious setting. For her baby there must be some eternal nursery where he could continue to flourish. But the Island would certainly have adopted him. It would have a place for dead little children behind those walls.

Two of her children had disappeared into that darkness. Neither had she loved well. Between Camilo and herself there had always been distance, fear, alienation—she being as reserved as he. With Rafael, warmth, affection, unexpected life, salvation, but where was his mother when he . . . ?

Perhaps because she had neither seen his dead body nor had attended his burial, she felt as if the child were still there and they were playing hide-and-seek, or blind-goat, a game in which she would grope her way around, trying to touch her son once more, her angel, but touching only emptiness.

Camilo, however, had made his death visible to everyone, with no ambiguity. Could the terrible zone of darkness where he now walked be brighter than Mother's garden, brighter than the room with the golden light? If one really concentrated, one could comprehend it.

Camilo, in his new reality. But where was it?

I am going to end up loving Death as much as he did, Renata thought. I am going to discover that after all only Death is certain, only Death exists, always waiting, still. We are but a breath of air in the dark, a flight that terminates in the womb of Death, the only reality.

V

Renata was lying on the sofa as she often did, with nothing to occupy her, when Clara phoned to tell her that Camilo had been hurt falling off a horse at the farm and that he would arrive at Mother's house within the hour. The call shook her out of her lethargy. Her sister-in-law's voice, always impersonal, was now strident, she was talking too loudly and too fast.

Renata didn't believe it. She hadn't even known that her son was at the farm. What was he doing in that detestable place? Two days ago the twins had been at Mother's house where they usually stayed.

"But he doesn't know how to ride," she had protested weakly, as if this would change something. Clara had already hung up. Renata took a taxi, and Clara was waiting for her at the door, outwardly calm, with the face of a made-up doll. Doesn't she ever lose her composure? Renata wondered, and then began to worry about her daughter. She still thought that Camilo's accident had been minor—but Carolina, so nervous, so close to her brother . . .

"Have they told the girl?" she asked.

"Mother went upstairs, but I don't think that she'll mention anything yet."

Mother came down a little later, saying that she had found Carolina sitting on the bed, drowsy. Had she heard anything downstairs?

Carolina had looked at her vacantly and had said, "I feel so strange, Mother . . ."

"How do you mean, strange?"

"Like I'm going to die."

The old lady had talked to her, reassured her, told her to lie down. Perhaps she would sleep a little.

"She seems wary of something, she senses something," said Mother, looking more than ever like an old cloth witch, with yellow hair and a big red dress.

Renata's heart skipped a beat. "It's always the same thing. One of them gets hurt, the other bleeds . . ."

And the three of them had the same thought: What would happen to Carolina if Camilo were gone?

When the two men finally brought him into the house, carrying him in their arms, he had just died. They set him down on the living room sofa. Renata tried to hold his head. His eyes were slightly open, but there was nothing behind them. Dull, opaque, like the eyes of the farm animals that died, that bothered her so much.

"So many deaths," she had always said, and Martin used to laugh without understanding.

"My God, my God!" she screamed. "My God, what happened, my son, what happened?"

Suddenly the tide of love broke loose in her, a hopeless, desperate, animal love. And she kissed him on his face, bloodying herself in his blood.

She kept crying out to him, "My son, my son! . . ." but he didn't respond.

62

After a while her grief made her numb. She had reached the limits of her endurance, and had remained there, floating, semiconscious. She could not suffer more than she was suffering now, she could not suffer more.

Then, while the men were still arranging the body on the sofa, not knowing what to do next, trying to explain what had happened, they were rocked by another crisis. They heard Carolina sobbing upstairs, wailing, finally screaming. One of the maids hurried in with towels and a bowl of water. Someone said, "She'll have to be tranquilized."

The scream stayed in the air, dissolving slowly, the voice thick with suffering in the thick air of the house, thick like thick milk, muddy waters, algae, jellyfish, slime.

After leaving Carolina upstairs sedated by the shot, Mother came down and paced back and forth, talking without pause. Martin . . . and where was Martin? He was on his way, it would take him two hours to get there. She was also worried about Clara, who in her mind was still a child, Clara had bad nerves, the shock would hurt her.

Clara had fled to the other side of the living room, where she sat on the sofa, absorbed in doing nothing.

Later, their hands shaking so much that they were almost incapacitated, Mother and Renata had taken Camilo's clothes off, to try to clean him up.

His clothes were filthy, his thin body smelled of a well, a basement.

By the time Martin arrived, Camilo had already embarked in his casket. They lighted candles, friends showed up, night fell. The news of the tragic death had spread quickly. People entered the house uncertainly, cautiously, as if stalking Death—Death, where is Death, who will one day take me too?

Martin suddenly rushed into the living room, then stopped abruptly, crying out, "But how did this happen, how did this happen?"

Then he went on, "Why did you do this to me, Son?" and Renata saw that he was stunned, enraged.

He embraced Renata awkwardly, with a dry sob, and then held Clara and Mother for many minutes. The three of them wept together, weeping and talking all at the same time, wanting to know, wanting to explain. Renata standing alone, off to one side. Finally all three grew quiet, all at the same time.

Martin then walked back and forth through the living room, sighing, moaning, sobbing tearlessly. He was a man accustomed to giving orders. In Death's territory he was impotent, as helpless and poor as anyone else. He clenched his fists, as if wanting to fight with Death, who more powerful than he had robbed him of his son before he was able to understand him or even, perhaps, to love him.

Renata and Martin automatically sat down on either side of the casket. The expression of bewilderment in their eyes changed little by little, his to a dark restlessness, hers to hurt and uncertainty.

In the casket between his parents, in the light, Camilo's face showed surprise, astonishment, as it had since the moment of death. He hid behind this mask in order to die better, undisturbed, and to learn the gesture, the face, the voice, the role he was to play in his new existence.

The wake was his opening night.

For Renata, too, meeting Martin under those circumstances had reopened wounds. Her wounds had not healed well, and every movement inflamed them further. At one point she went upstairs to see her daughter, walking slowly, holding onto the rail like someone very old or very sick. But in the twins' room Carolina looked asleep, and Renata didn't disturb her.

She returned to the living room and once again took up her post. Husband and wife separated by their dead son, as if

64

by a river of darkness. From time to time they got up for somebody to embrace them, in grief. Tears, handkerchiefs, frightened eyes. Renata thought about all of her children constantly, but particularly Camilo. Had she been too hard on him, separating him and his sister to preserve their identities, demanding that at least they sleep separately? Should she have not gone along with Martin? Should she have tried to get closer to them, to understand them better, to be warmer toward them, more affectionate, to cultivate a happiness in them that she didn't have in her? Love was so difficult!

Difficult, because it was impossible to overcome one's own nature. She had really tried. Every time there was a conflict, she would decide that Martin was overstating the problem. The twins were just innocent children, she would tell herself confidently. But deep down she felt that the twins had something dark and secret between them.

Camilo and Carolina, strange double being born of her womb, double by mistake, her defect, her fault. But Renata didn't know how to intervene, or how to correct the mistake.

She knew so little about her own children. They had been raised by nursemaids, by Mother and by Clara. By nobody, really. Two slender plants that someone had tied together so that they could support each other as they grew.

Sometimes when he was small Renata felt closer to Camilo. She remembered that he liked to hear her play. She would often see him in a corner very quietly listening to her, his eyes glistening with tears, and she would be moved. But soon she'd forget it, immersed as she was in her own problems.

Once, but only once, after she had not played for several months, he had asked her, "Aren't you ever going to play again?" And when she said no, Camilo turned away from her and went off, never again to bring up the subject.

Perhaps Clara knew the twins better than she did. When they were little Clara would take them up to her room and play with them, when they were older they would discuss books and magazines together. She liked to dress them in ancient mardi-gras costumes from bygone festivals. Having carefully made up their faces, she would parade the twins in front of Mother in the living room: two sensual concubines, two melancholy clowns. Renata would look away.

Maybe Clara knew about their invasions of Ella's room, but Renata lacked the courage to ask her. Her sister-in-law would look at her, smiling, saying: What harm was there in it? It was only an invalid's room. Ella was not an animal. Or was she? Clara would ask with her eyes wide open, like a child, like an insane person, like a savant.

Night was falling, the tide coming in. Voices clamoring: Death, where is she, where did she carry the boy she has just chosen? Where, and how?

Martin was asking himself: What has snatched my son from me and left in his place this empty thing whose being I can no longer reach?

Above everything else it was an insult. A person who commits suicide is always accusing someone. Had he been a bad father? Should he have been more affectionate, more understanding? It had always been difficult to get close to Camilo, a quiet child, distant, resistant to his father's overtures.

What had he been feeling those final few days, hours? It was terrible to think that the last time they met—Martin could hardly remember the occasion—there could have been signals in Camilo's eyes, pleas, something that might have revealed his trouble. And his father hadn't known how to see it.

66

Now Camilo had put himself into death's space, and his yellow eyes turned back, sad, accusing. He had always been a lonely child, without friends, without interests, finding pleasure only in his sister, in a strange relationship.

He killed himself to punish me, Martin thought. But I did the best I could.

Yes, he had done his best, everyone always did one's best. He had worn himself out giving all he could to the family. Often, while the others were relaxing, he would leave the house, speed along the road to the farm, take care of the chores that actually belonged to the hired help, and mingle with them, for he wanted to prove that he too was capable of farm work. He wanted these concrete activities to block out the unhappiness of his inner life. In the city office, he kept his calendar so busy that he had almost no time to think.

But he did think. Renata's face was with him day and night, unreciprocated love. She had talked to him of her loneliness when they had first known each other. And he had been impressed, for no woman had ever revealed her intimate life to him before, the life that lies deepest within, the life of the soul. Renata's was a solitary soul.

Yet when he married her and showed his adoration for her, she began to be unhappy. She fled from him like someone who kisses and departs. . . . And she spent her years of marriage departing and returning, departing and returning, the gap between them increasing with each quarrel.

"Why can't we be happy," Martin asked one day, holding her by her shoulders, shaking her as if to wake her from a bad dream.

"It's not your fault," she said, and then almost in a whisper, turning her face away, "I'm neurotic, that's all."

Was she neurotic? Yes, she was a complicated woman. Clara had sometimes hinted that Renata made life too complicated. Mother never criticized her, Martin never heard her rebuke her, Mother always wanted to understand and forgive.

He hadn't accomplished anything by being good, doing things right, Martin was convinced. And even after their final separation, he kept on suffering from his love for her, which had left a sad and ugly sore that was beginning to throb again that night.

And his son. He had failed to make him a wholesome young man. In Martin's eyes, Camilo's inclination toward femininity, his attachment to Carolina were dangerous. The boy apparently didn't like his father, he never wanted to get involved in any of his activities, and he had an unsatisfactory relationship with his mother. Sometimes, when Camilo was still a child, Martin had surprised him listening to her play the piano, in hiding. Renata didn't like to play for anyone. If she had to do so she played mechanically. Only in solitude did she liberate her passion and her pain through her music. And this was how she was playing when Camilo watched in the darkness, his eyes glistening. Who was Camilo?

Martin had been afraid that his son might want to be an artist too.

All of that irritated Martin, fed his suspicions, worried him. Growing up, Camilo intimidated his father, the boy was so quiet, cold. Delicate, like his mother, impractical, immersed in books and conversations with his sister, always listening to records, to classical music, the same music Renata used to listen to in private.

More recently Martin had decided that it was time for Camilo to have a girl friend. He thought about discussing the matter with him, but they saw each other rarely. There was no trace of any camaraderie between them that might permit such a dialogue.

"Don't you have a girl friend yet?" Martin would ask. And Camilo, raising his eyes from his book, perhaps with one hand absentmindedly playing with a curl of his sister's hair, would turn his delicate face towards him and gaze at him as if he were scrutinizing a strange animal.

After Mother had gone upstairs with Carolina, Martin returned to the far side of the living room to watch Renata. He was still her captive. Threads, rags, loose bandages of an unresolved love kept him tied to her. His heart had been damaged by love, and he had thought that the ache was hate.

Threatened by sleep, Martin rubbed his eyes. He remembered events from his children's infancy, disappointments, his frustrated efforts to get closer to them, to understand them, to make them love him. And to love them.

When they were six years old, Martin had planned a party, a picnic at the farm. Perhaps he wanted to put on a good show, to do something for the children he vaguely rejected.

He ordered a great surprise for after lunch—a pony for Camilo. Saddle, ropes, everything small and perfect, all that would make any boy happy. Any boy but Camilo. The story, now ancient, became a source of jokes for friends, a source of fights for the family. Camilo hated the farm, he feared animals, he had never been on a horse alone, although a couple of times his father had ignored his cries of horror and had taken the boy riding with him.

Perhaps Martin expected to force things to be right. That was the way he was. He wanted to force Camilo to like everything that was important to him, so that he could prove to his friends that his son was not queer.

Seeing the horse, Camilo tried to hide among the guests, but his father's powerful hands seized him and set him on the saddle, even while he was still struggling to get away. Soon the adults stopped laughing, they became embarrassed. Camilo was screaming, barely staying in the saddle. Martin hit him twice, and Carolina, sitting on Renata's lap, cried as much as her brother.

Flushed with rage and humiliation, Martin led the horse by the reins in a slow turn around the house in sight of everyone. Camilo on top, holding on to keep from falling, his crying become a high-pitched wail.

After that day the already strained ties between father and son were practically severed. Camilo would approach Martin with his head lowered, as if to defend himself from a possible attack.

"He likes only his cows," he said to his mother one day, when she had asked him to be nicer to his father.

At the same time Camilo seemed to brighten with the affection of Carolina. Like those animals that work so frantically to rebuild their home after it has been destroyed, the twins labored day by day to weave a world of their own.

VI

The world outside is gone, the woman noticed, her face pressed against the window pane. The fog swallowed everything, shapes and colors, it isolated the house in a white silence.

When young she had dreaded foggy nights, because of being afraid to stay closed up in the house alone. Anyone looking for her would be unable to find her. There were no maps or guides that would locate her.

But that night she felt protected, because if misfortune wanted her it too would get lost.

With her finger she wrote her name on the misty pane: Clara. Underneath, a large fancy P.

Then turning back to the middle of the room, she opened her arms, lifted up her head, and, completely naked, began to dance, slowly, sensually, with her breasts swaying and her silver hair falling around her shoulders giving off glints of light.

Friends of the family thought that Clara could still get married. In her youth she had had many suitors, and even now she still had a few. A beautiful woman, carefully made up, with gray hair that set off her fair skin.

There was something no one understood about her life. There was talk of an unhappy love affair. Weeks on end she would stay home closed up in the house, dusting the furniture and preparing special dishes for Mother or for her nephew and niece. But every afternoon when she came down before dinner, she would dress as if she were going to a party. From time to time, she had tea with old school friends, but she never seemed to be really there.

A falsely polished surface of glass. . . . But it was not glass, it was water, from whose depths emerged bubbles of restlessness. She had spent time in rest clinics, everyone knew.

In her dark eyes was there a flash of insanity?

Clara interrupted her sensual dance and pounded her stomach, now beginning to get flabby, with her fists.

"Coward! coward!" she exclaimed in despair. She sat on the edge of the bed without getting dressed. She remembered the nightmare of the night before, always the same. She was standing on the edge of a cliff or on the outside ledge of a high window. Something was sucking her down, sucking her by her feet, something irresistible, repulsive. She knew that if she let herself go she would never return. Was it pleasure or death?

Her teeth began to chatter. She pulled up a blanket, covered her naked body, drew up her legs, and leaned against a pillow by the wall. Locks of hair clung to her damp forehead.

Then sobbing, she cried out, "Why do you do this to me?"

What she could not get over in her grotesque history was his cowardice. He had tossed the stone of his strange passion into the placid waters of her body, of her soul, and had gone away, leaving a whirlpool that would not end.

At the time Clara was an adolescent, physically more fragile than Martin, who was strong. She was barely opening up to life when that man entered her hidden forest and planted madness there. And he ran away.

Other times she would think: He loves me, yes, of course he loves me, he needs me and he will return. Didn't I do what he asked me to do?

She would spin fantasies, and have her periods of frenzy then. She would change clothes all the time, take her makeup off and put it back on, go downstairs dressed for a party. He would come soon, that very night, that very instant.

After such a period she would be in a state of confusion. Martin and Mother would put her in a clinic where she could sleep, rest.

As the years went by she forgot his face, she discovered that there is no truth. Only lies. In her mind her suitors, momentary infatuations, always had the same face, his, not real. And she fled before knowing them. What did they want from her? Was that what love was?

Little by little she constructed for herself the lover whom she could create and uncreate at will, whom she secretly called the Priest.

He will return, she told herself again and again. He will return. It made sense for him to return. The thought helped her get through difficult times, like that night, when a dead adolescent boy lay downstairs. In some ways he and Carolina had been her children, her siblings, her companions in loneliness. Now Camilo had killed himself, and she, irrationally holding on to her faceless, nameless lover, felt that she would fall apart once more. Fear was blowing through her, death. Death now had an identity—it was the face and the body that looked like Camilo in the casket.

He was still warm that afternoon when she touched him, and said under her breath, "It is over."

Now he must be as cold as a doll of porcelain.

He had wanted to know, Clara was certain. She was familiar with the game of death that the twins had secretly played when they were little, she knew about their nightly visits to the forbidden room, Camilo dragging his sister by the hand. The two, pale and disheveled, would go to make love to Evil who breathed through the invalid's lips.

Camilo had finally found what he had so long sought, now he lived, loved, made discoveries elsewhere. He had freed himself of his obsession, of his impossible bond with Carolina.

Drawn up into a ball in bed, still feeling cold, Clara realized that Camilo had gone to die at the place he hated most, the farm, where he went only when his father ordered him to go or, rarely, when he wanted to please Mother. Since Martin had left, Camilo had not gone there.

What had compelled him to go that afternoon? What had pulled him there? Who had been leaning ingratiatingly against the farm gate with open arms? Something that both repelled and attracted. Like the room? Like love?

In the living room, Martin remembered the children's sixth birthday, their party, the gift for Camilo, the tears that still haunted him in nightmares.

His son had vindicated himself, dying *that* death at *that* place.

The men who brought him in that afternoon told Martin everything they knew, but he wanted to know more. What had the boy said? How was he acting? Why hadn't they stopped him?

And he made them explain everything again and again, interrupting them with exclamations of incredulity and rage, interrupting them with sobs.

In the car Mother had given the twins a few months earlier on their eighteenth birthday, Camilo had raced madly out to the farm, arriving in the middle of the afternoon. He had stopped near the courtyard, had stepped out looking disoriented, and had asked for the wildest horse.

Surprised, the men had pointed to an animal in a corral nearby.

"That one is the Devil himself, nobody can ride him."

Although they had noticed Camilo's nervousness, the farm hands could not have imagined what was about to happen. They observed aghast the scene that unfolded in seconds: Camilo ran to the fence, leaped over it with energy they hadn't realized he possessed, and jumped on the horse, shouting, hanging on desperately to his back, clutching his mane, burying his face in the mane.

The animal reared, galloped a short way, bucked, threw Camilo to the ground, then trampled on the still body. Camilo had cracked his head open on the rocks.

It was difficult to calm the animal down, to pull him away. Camilo, unconscious, was barely breathing as they drove him to the city in the truck.

The men told Martin that it didn't look like an accident. Camilo had sought to die, had thrown himself onto Death.

It was the flanks of Death he had held, yelling with hatred, or with fear, and in his fit of rage and fright, he had soiled his clothes with blood and feces. He died at the moment they arrived at Mother's house.

The men didn't say that it was Camilo who emitted the odor that he had hated at the farm, the odor that had attracted him to Ella's room, where, surrounded by life's leavings, life's debris, so often he had had a foreboding of Death waiting in the corner in ambush, delaying treacherously the final embrace.

Nobody remembered having forbidden the twins to enter. Everybody in the house knew that only Mother, Martin, and occasionally Clara went in. Once in a while a maid was hired to help, to clean the room more thoroughly, sometimes to turn the invalid in the bed on days when Mother was too tired. Nobody else. Even those who did enter the room didn't say much when they came out. Perhaps they didn't even look, perhaps they wanted to forget. Perhaps they had nothing to tell.

For the twins, the room was a raw sore to be covered up and not touched, a sore that kept on throbbing no matter what. Perhaps they spent their time imagining what might be in there—a rare animal, a strange plant, a creature from the marsh, sending signals through the house at any hour. They were afraid. Or were they afraid?

At night when they slept at Mother's house, they would stare at the dark in their own bedroom. Was the Thing living in the closed room also awake?

One day they uncovered the secret. There within it, they contemplated still waters and guessed the depths. There were rumblings in the mire.

Perhaps their curiosity had resulted from a threat, such as: If you don't do what I want, I'll lock you up with her in the dark. . . . Could someone have said that?

The twins had visited the room for the first time after Mother had accidentally left the key in the door. Thus they began their long, drawn-out, elaborate discovery of their power. They had unlimited power before that almost inanimate carcass, the Mollusk.

"Can she talk?" Carolina asked. Once her eyes had be-

76

come accustomed to the darkness, she could make out the thing on the bed.

"I don't know," Camilo said, more interested in the disproportionate size of the head.

The invalid made a low rasping noise.

"Does she have a name?" Carolina asked in a thin voice.

"I don't know."

Suddenly the creature let out a howl, and the twins gasped, and fled, their eyes big. But they knew they had to return to that room.

Camilo discovered another key in Mother's room. Now they were owners of the cave. But sometimes they let months pass without going into it, enjoying the situation. Enjoying what?

They built up their courage with each visit, they wanted Ella to react to them. They explored her, got close, touched her with a finger. After a while they felt courageous enough to lift the sheets.

Sometimes, when the twins dared to go beyond that, two astonished beady eyes, black and cruel, watched them.

For Camilo and Carolina the creature imprisoned in the room in such prolonged agony was connected in some way with Clara preparing herself for a love postponed forever. One day they asked her.

"What are you waiting for, always looking so pretty?"

Clara answered, "I'm waiting for my fiancé."

"What's his name?"

"The Priest."

And the three of them sat there listening, waiting, as if in the middle of that absence he might appear, with his black cassock, with a face made up of many faces, and with a name that Clara no longer recalled.

Seated on the bed, she tried hard to remember his nose, his eyes, his mouth. What was the color of his hair, the shape of

77

his head? She remembered only his hands, large, dark hands stroking piano keys as if they were her body.

Naked under the blanket, she felt again what she so much wanted and feared, sexual passion. It happened periodically. Pernicious desire for a man without identity, who had given her ecstasy and had abandoned her without explanation. The fervor that once consumed her had cooled to resignation.

Lethargy had taken over, the routine of getting dressed up without knowing why, quiet madness, useless love, purposeless life.

Clara threw off the suffocating blanket. She looked at the window where the letters of her name were beginning to run.

Sometimes she thought that this was all God's revenge. The Priest had sinned, she had helped him sin, and now God was punishing them by keeping them apart. The Priest. This Priest of rough cassock and soft tongue, who smelled of something forbidden, the man scent that perturbed her the first time he approached her. Shouldn't all Priests be asexual?

Before that occasion she had had a few adolescent infatuations that revealed to her her body's hidden forces. But the Priest rushed into her life like a hurricane, and he disturbed the deep waters still sleeping within her at a time when she did not yet have the capacity to recompose herself. What year had it been, what day? Who had made the first overture? Had the cassock touched her satin blouse for the first time because she had bent over too much, or because he . . . ?

With each memory, with each daydream she had during her periods of frenzy, Clara changed their roles, alternated them, gave her fantasy a different form. But what happened had happened. The details didn't matter; it had happened and it had ripped her apart.

If Mother could have guessed what would happen, she certainly would not have invited the Priest for dinner, nor would she have shown him the old piano that nobody played

78

which she kept tuned and covered with an embroidered table-cloth. Perhaps everything had to happen this way, the termite-filled piano placed there by destiny, so that one day the Priest might come to caress its keys, awakening in her the flood of emotions that were never to climax, never to be controlled.

It is for me he plays, Clara thought with his first notes. She felt dizzy, light-headed, weak all over. It is for me, for me. She looked at his hands, large, sensitive, sensual hands, she wanted those hands to uncover her, instruct her, penetrate her. Afterwards she ran out of the living room in torment. Wasn't this a sin?

But every time he came, apparently to console Mother about Ella's condition, Clara stayed around. When she was alone she dreamed about him, weaving a mad, passionate love story.

One night they remained downstairs when Mother went up to help the invalid. Martin must have gone out, as Mother had insisted since his stepsister's accident that he try to amuse himself more, to keep from being depressed. The Priest played the piano. Clara leaned against the wall and listened. Then she sat down beside him on the piano bench, knowing he wouldn't send her away. Soon they were holding each other as if they were drowning, and struggling to survive.

There were other occasions in the silent house for ardent embraces, touches, glances at each other. Clara felt guilt and madness devouring her in the midst of flames.

One day, she dared to telephone him when Mother had stepped out.

"Come over now, I'm alone."

It had happened as quickly and as silently as in a silent movie, like a projection without sound on an opaque screen. That was how she always recalled it. She had locked the door to the music room, had lain on the sofa, and had said only, "Come here."

Between kisses and unconnected words, she had helped the Priest remove her blouse, her skirt. When she was almost naked he kissed and bit and licked her, and then suddenly stopped, holding her by the shoulders, looking at her with a strange expression.

And in the vulgar voice of a drunk, a voice not his, he made that unexpected request.

He was still completely dressed, locked into his black cassock, and she was almost naked in his arms.

"You only want to see it?" she had echoed him, suddenly cold and lucid, shrinking back, with her sex closing up, sore as a windflower touched by an acidic, frozen, noxious finger.

The Priest spoke with short gasps, staring at some point above Clara's head. It was not that he loved her or desired her—he had an obsession, an illness that disturbed his soul. He needed to see, only to see. He didn't want to harm her, who was little more than a girl, who knew nothing about anything. What did she know about passion's torments? Because she was so sweet he had decided: She loves me and she is innocent, and I won't commit the terrible sin.

He hoped that if he could *see* it he would free himself. He would be able to placate the fierce hunger that gnawed at him within. It would be almost a vision, a mystical vision—he had used that word, Clara was sure, yes, that word, and had almost made her laugh like a mad woman. Mystical fever: to look at a woman's sex. If he were to look at Clara, young and sinless, he would be contemplating the fountain of life, and that couldn't be sinful.

Clara understood their conflict. She had constructed a love affair, the Priest had had a fever, she had invented a man, he had suffered a delirium. He was seeking in the chasm of life a salvation she could not give him.

Was he mentally ill? Clara had heard of manias, and had heard that some men had manias. The Priest needed to look at her. Was it to exorcise some demon sucking his soul?

80

Then she began understanding, and in seconds understood, that she had to be his mother.

She felt simultaneously both profound shame and strange joy. The excitement gone, she felt heavy and cold, but also maternal. She neither spat in his face, nor laughed at his request, nor insulted him. She loved him in that instant with another kind of love, a love so rare that she would never find it again in her own coiled soul. Was it sordid? Or sublime? She couldn't say.

She yielded. Quickly and graciously, she took off her panties. Clenching her teeth, out of shame, she spread her legs and, taking his tormented face in her hands, guided him, like a blind man, toward her innocent and sad sex.

Clara never saw him again. At first she thought about dying. She could not absorb what had happened, she could not accept it, her world was falling apart and she could not put it back together. She had periods of depression and rebellion— she thought she was ill. She could not speak to anyone, she felt strange, mad. She thought about killing herself when Martin told her casually that the Priest who used to visit who played the piano so well had been transferred. Far, far away.

After a few months of depression, a few months of deceiving Martin and Mother about the reasons for her change, Clara threw herself into a series of inconsequential courtships. In the years thereafter, when her suitors spoke of love, she would wonder what love really was, and what a man really was.

She wanted to be loved, yet she couldn't tolerate others' loving her. If they said, "I love you," she would close herself off and become aggressive, hostile, and dangerous. Gazing with expressionless eyes on every suitor she had, she would hurt them, for fear that they would hurt her.

She distanced herself from reality. She rocked herself to sleep with her dream. Her love was impossible. But in moments of lucidity, she would ask herself: Are there really impossible loves or are there only cowardly hearts?

That night, with Camilo downstairs, she was very upset. It was not only love that threatened her, not only loneliness that gnawed at her, there were things moving in the dark, in the fog. Once again she tried to compose herself, to understand her own life. She got herself together and then fell apart, again and again and again.

From her fantasy she nearly always got pleasure and warmth, and her own precarious inner peace. She did not let herself suffer while awaiting that ghost lover. I don't want to suffer any more, she cried, I don't want to suffer any more. And she found consolation caressing herself.

She got up, went over to the window, and with her hand rubbed out the rest of her name on the wet pane. Once again in bed, she could not see that the large P had not yet disappeared.

 *Third Part: Thanatos*

To live is the dream of a dream.
To awaken is to be elsewhere.

RILKE

VII

Dead, Renata's son began to occupy her heart like someone making himself comfortable in a room. Now you're more nearly mine, she thought. I shall give you the milk of my grief, the milk of my contemplation of your death. . . .

Camilo's mind, Camilo's memory, would hold no more fear, no more suspicion. She knew he was imprisoned within the frame of that Island, where everything was defined forever.

Nothing could change him any more. All his secrets kept secret forever, Camilo lay defenseless before them for all to see. Free of the compulsion to be Carolina, perhaps he could now be his mother's son. He had arrived at the place he had sought, the Other had answered his plea.

Renata noticed that Martin was watching her, but she no longer cared. She touched the edge of the casket, as if to steady a boat in the water. She rested her head on her arm and stared at the shadows on the floor. She felt dizzy. Suddenly, in the darkness at her feet—as happened so often when she let down her guard—there appeared the round happy face of Angel Rafael.

I neglected the twins then, always carrying him around, she started thinking. With that son everything was so different. Still she hadn't nursed him, she couldn't, she was afraid to try. But all her hopes for reconstructing her life, for regaining her inner wholeness, for finally learning to love and to be generous and to liberate herself, she placed on him.

Watching over her son, she almost forgot her piano. Her life with Martin improved, they both handled their new happiness as if it were a flower of glass.

The twins, withdrawing even more after their brother's birth, grew up in the absentminded care of Mother, in whose house they spent most of their time.

Slowly order came to Renata's life, the possibility of being happy.

But one day the demon returned to haunt that peace. He pulled Renata's skirt, caressed her face, wrapped himself around her heart, stirred up her mind. She could neither eat, sleep, nor play with her baby, unless she could again play the piano. And not just casually, to please some visitor or to distract herself, but passionately, to expose the depths of her soul.

So she would sometimes send Rafael to Mother's house with the nursemaid, and then alone in the apartment mount her piano, trembling with pleasure. In those hours, as she felt revive the person she once had been, Renata remembered Miguel, who would have loved her in spite of everything, who would not have wanted a separation, who had cried the last time they had been together. His face floated over the piano in front of her.

Deep down Renata knew that not even Rafael could serve as a substitute for the vocation she had betrayed.

On one of those afternoons Clara was playing with

Rafael in her room, planning to take him afterwards to the garden, when the twins showed up. So they decided to go down all together. But Clara remembered a new magazine she wanted to take, and she hurried back, leaving Rafael at the top of the stairs between his brother and his sister, who were supposed to hold him tightly by the hand.

Clara was just coming out of her room when she heard a muffled thud, and then another, and another, something rolling down the stairs. A final thud, and a weak cry, like a cat's meow.

Then silence.

No one could explain how Angel Rafael had rolled all the way down the stairs, to crack his head on the landing. On her knees beside him, Clara had glimpsed Camilo and Carolina standing still at the top, silent and pale, holding hands as if to help each other.

Martin, out of his mind with grief, spanked them, but accomplished nothing.

They would say only, "I don't know."

Renata did not go to the funeral, the shock sent her to bed for days. When she finally did get up, she was a spent, broken woman. Martin moved to the farm for good, and when he needed to stay in the city he spent the night either in his office or, more rarely, at Mother's house. His relationship with Camilo and Carolina was reduced to occasional meetings. Actually the twins avoided their father, separated from him by a silent, terrible suspicion floating in the air between them, an accusation.

And he and his wife were separated by an unasked yet logical question: Renata, what were you doing when our son . . . ?

Martin aged with Rafael's death. His eyes lost their luster. After recovering, he threw himself into his work, lived alone, had affairs. A disillusioned man.

Renata never played the piano again. Martin sold the one

in the apartment as well as the one on the farm, and, in spite of Clara's protests, even the worm-eaten one at Mother's house.

Everybody had left: the last visitor had drowned in the fog.

Renata and Martin, lone spectators to the gradual transformation of Camilo, who was silhouetted in the light in the middle of the living room, like an actor.

Every hour, his expression showed more tension, more alertness. No longer terror, not a smile, it showed an intense effort to learn.

The night of truth, Renata thought. Your truth now, my son, is to inhabit that other side, where I may not yet go.

Death, the game that fascinated him. Renata knew that when they were little her children had had a strange way of playing. Would she have been able to keep them from playing that game if they were almost always alone together? Besides, she was always tired. Comfortable knowing that her children had each other, she had allowed them to grow up on their own.

Now Camilo was dead, he had died a dirty death of tears and fright and the detested stench of horse sweat. The eyes of the Devil rolling in enormous sockets.

Like a murderous lover, the horse had trampled Camilo even after he was on the ground.

"He died an animal," said one of the maids, carrying off his clothes to wash them.

If he could speak the dead boy would say, "I wanted to understand why I was born divided in two. I wanted to comprehend the enigma of Life and all I found was the face of Death, which I'll try to learn now."

He had had to die—he had not been content with the pale reflection of light in Carolina's eyes. His existence had been torture, insufficient because he could become complete

88

only by also being Carolina, excessive because being partially his sister he felt everything doubly, he lived his own experience doubly, and that of his other half.

He needed to know. More restless than Carolina, more tense, more intense, he needed to reach perfection, wholeness, to arrive at the paradise that defied him and called him and slowly opened to devour him.

Growing up, he had made the painful discovery that to touch each other souls needed bodies. He tried to communicate this to Carolina, but did she understand? Did she have an answer, a solution? He didn't want to scare her or hurt her, Carolina, the trace, the shadow that followed.

Immature, almost childish, they were satisfied with fraternal caresses, a kiss on the cheek, a touch of the hand, they were satisfied with breathing in the same rhythm, sleeping in the same room when they could. Each contemplating the other's face, multiplying their questions. They liked to be together in silence, to walk in the garden, to read or study the same book, thinking thoughts that became the same thought.

At times they laughed for no reason, alleviating their constant anxiety, they laughed in the pleasure of knowing: You exist.

Correct but absent-minded in their daily routine. Almost immune to their father's hostility, their mother's bad moods. She had been a great pianist, Mother sometimes said. Now she didn't play any more, but she had once played often, and by herself. She had made them leave and had locked herself up to play, as if she found playing in front of her children embarrassing, constraining. They felt they disturbed her. So they withdrew into each other.

Some day something had to happen. They could foresee it, though they couldn't say what it would be. Were they to fuse themselves into one? Life split in two was transitory, impossible to maintain.

But in recent months they had avoided each other to keep from revealing what worried them both, the painful questions: What will become of us? Why aren't you enough for me?

Camilo had started bringing someone he knew to Mother's house. Camilo, who didn't have friends, had found a beautiful boy, a young man, with a robust body and a slightly vulgar laugh. He fascinated the twins, who were so withdrawn, with his casual, carefree lack of concern for things in life.

They hardly spoke of him, though they usually discussed everything with each other, bringing order to their world by talking. But about this stranger they said nothing.

If he could speak the dead boy would say, "He just showed up on a street corner, and I thought he might be the solution to our problem. There was something in his face, in his gesture, in the movement of his eyes, that caught me. What was it? What did he remind me of? Who was it who one day . . . ?"

Camilo played the death game with Carolina. He searched the golden well of her eyes, he searched his own solitude, asking: What am I? Who am I? But in his process of searching he multiplied his questions: How could he live with only Carolina? With nothing to take him out of this cold, silent existence.

Could he take a single step away from her? Did he have the right to do so? Would his leaving cripple her?

If he could speak the dead boy would say, "For the first time we started lying to each other. Each of us wanted to be alone with him, the Intruder. Why? To do what? We didn't know. For the first time I couldn't get to sleep in her room, because I was aware the whole time that she was there. Or was I restless because of him?"

If the Guest fell in love with both Camilo and Carolina,

did that prove that they were one, the same? And if they both, at the same time . . . ? But he couldn't put the fantasy into words.

By way of the Other, through his madness and his pleasure, could they finally become one forever? Or would they find some form of liberation in the end?

Camilo was wide awake. Carolina walked in a trance.

All that was to happen was there before they had ever been born, when they were still in the seed, even before the seed—when Death first signals, and we fall into the world, coming out from under her cloak. Death later signals a second time, and we return to her bosom, which drapes us in darkness and damp.

Camilo was disintegrating, consumed with passion. Is it he whose breath moves my body, or is it she, Carolina?

She too felt suddenly strange—temporary, provisional.

Death, naked seductress, came into their group.

Camilo, who had once been calm, whose emotions had once been weak, felt now like a raging bull defending the cows at the farm, ready to attack, scratch, bite and kill.

In an atmosphere of heavy sensuality, the game lasted for weeks. Practically ignoring the brother, who was irritatingly sweet, who fixed thirsty eyes on him, the young man wanted to have fun with Carolina. But Camilo's feminine face, repeating his sister's so strangely, disturbed him.

One morning the young man went to bed with Carolina in her room at Mother's house. Suddenly aware that he was their pawn in a frightening game he didn't understand, he penetrated her furiously, without affection, as if to desecrate her, and she opened up in pain, moaning.

In his pleasure he felt terror at his own ambiguity: in the naked face of Carolina he had wanted to kiss and bite the face of Camilo. That was what it had all been about, the whole time. Hunting her and being hunted by her, he was really chasing her brother and being chased by him, and it was he whom he had just raped in a profoundly perverted act.

Carolina, in a long spasm beneath his body, had seen in a flash: I am Camilo. To him who is on top of me, I am Camilo. Is that what we really wanted?

And she realized too that Camilo had offered himself to the Other in her, seeking through her, in the pleasure that was anguish and pain, something that would take him beyond everything, past their searching, out of their boundaries. Leaving her alone forever.

Then, turning aside her head, feeling that she would die in the contraction, she saw Camilo leaning against the door-jamb, gazing at himself exposed upon the sheets.

But Camilo hadn't had a key and Carolina had locked the door.

Maybe Camilo had collected, in addition to the key to Ella's room, the keys to all the rooms of the house. And he would often snoop around without anyone noticing, secretly entering rooms in the middle of the night to watch people sleep, observing the cords of life in them in the pulley of time operated by the bony hands of the Lady he so much wanted to unmask.

If he could speak the dead boy would say: "At the bottom of the well I found united Life and Death, masculine and feminine, the I and the Other, devouring each other like the serpent that swallows his own tail. From darkness and insanity Death leaped out, opening her arms wide—prostitute, damsel, promise, damnation. Drunk with mystery, she called me, and I had to know: Whose bosom awaits me? What silence? What new language?"

The whole way to the farm Camilo knew: Someone, someone I once loved, awaits. Faceless, nameless, intact, awaiting me.

Mounting the demon, the smell of his own semen mixed

92

with that of sweat and animal gases, he howled with pleasure and fear, hatred and victory. He expelled feces and
urine, and finally fell into the embrace where he would be
only Camilo, dissolved in beauty, liberated in a water without banks, become at once boat, passenger, and the deep.

VIII

"Holy shit!" Mother said aloud, as she sat alone in her room on the bed, with her legs apart, her swollen feet off the floor.

It had been an agonizing day. Camilo's death, Carolina's strange despair, Renata's grief, Martin's bewilderment. And Clara's serenity, at least she was no trouble, she was in a period of calm, Clara, who resisted growing up, her companion, with whom, as the years went by, she had woven a domestic life outside reality of little details, intrigues, memories, but never plans for the future.

In her nightgown Mother removed her makeup with cream-soaked cotton. She had already unglued her false eyelashes, exposing naked, sad eyes amid folds of wrinkled skin. She still wore her wig. She washed her face carelessly, without glancing in the mirror. For her it was no longer a ritual of preserving her youth but rather a bothersome daily necessity. She didn't even know why she kept fixing herself up after she'd gotten old the way she did when she was forty, when she was strong and full of hope. She felt vaguely ridiculous, but she had never had time to pause to verify for herself that she had aged. She just kept going out of habit. On such a path as hers through life to pause was dangerous, she could start thinking too much. And if her control gave way, what would burst forth from within?

Mother did what she had to do without pondering it, she would do it all till the end. She joked: On Judgment Day I shall appear with a medicine bottle in one hand and Ella's dirty diaper in the other.

She laughed with a little snort, and her sagging breasts shook.

Mother was sad and weary. And lonely. In the first few years of her daughter's illness, many friends and relatives had come by to comfort her. Then one day without warning the hope she had nourished in spite of the doctor's skepticism vanished, and the certainty that Ella would not recover installed itself for good. Ella would get worse and sink deeper into that marasmus, she was already losing her senses, she would never return.

And friends visited her less and less frequently and relatives were busy and the doctors gave up, these days only an old family friend dropped by from time to time to give the same old prescriptions and check to see that Ella's benumbed life had not changed.

Ella dragged herself along like a great snail capable of covering only a few centimeters of the journey every day. But where was she headed?

Mother groaned. She had left some makeup on her face, an unhappy, aging clown's face.

If only Ella had gone instead of Camilo, she thought without remorse. Or if she had really died that day almost thirty years ago. How could one live in this condition for so long? If Ella had died, the only thing she'd have to care for now would be a clean, hygienic tomb with ivy planted around it and a picture in tones of sepia. Ella immortalized in her beauty at the age of twenty.

Ella, fruit of a drunken night, when Mother was young and happy. Ella had been happy too, and patient, complaining little of Mother's obvious favoritism for Clara and Martin. She was never any trouble, even that business with Martin was nothing serious.

Or was it?

Mother still held in her small, fat hand the dirty wad of cotton, lacking the energy to toss it in the waste basket.

Or was it?

Mother had always been crazy about Martin. She usually gave in to whatever he wanted, but that time she absolutely refused.

"She is your sister, and that's the end of the discussion."

They obeyed. There wasn't even time for great scenes. First there had been suspicion, gossip. Ella and Martin kissing each other in secret, Ella and Martin taking long walks on the farm, Ella and Martin locking themselves up in the sitting room of the city house. Tears, cries, orders, threats to send Ella away. Then suddenly, resolving everything, her fall brought a truce.

Afterwards Ella had almost thirty years to make demands on her mother. Often, when bending over the ruins of her daughter, tending to her repulsive needs, Mother thought: Is Ella getting even because I didn't love her enough? Or because I denied her Martin's love?

Did that soft, shapeless mass covered with scabs still think? With hatred? Rancor?

In her vile state, the invalid did and did not exist. She had a hard time breathing, her bodily functions never ceased.

Ella, a ship lost in the night, calling out. The large white cheek pressing the button. Could she be laughing at me? Mother wondered. Could she know that I always answer because I'm afraid not to? I never complain, never, because of fear.

"Never!" Mother said, her eyes moist. She cried, suddenly overcome by an awareness of her great deed, and by weariness. Why was Ella hanging on to that meaningless life?

"Never," she repeated. She slowly took off her wig to expose her round, almost bald head, the skull that was Ella's.

"Holy shit!" she said again, appreciating the company of her own voice. It had occurred to her that everyone in the house had a mania for falling.

Wasn't it weird? The death of Camilo . . . poor little Camilo . . . She wanted to hold him in her lap as she had done when he was small, but even then the boy wouldn't relax, or let himself go, love made him too vulnerable, he didn't want it. Poor Camilo.

Ella had fallen off the fence, Camilo had fallen off the horse, and also Angel Rafael. . . . Was it possible that the twins had not been able to hold on to him? Mother remembered Martin, carrying his dead baby through the house, howling, insane with grief, unable to admit that it was all over, the tenderness, the beauty, the innocence, the baby's life, all over . . .

Mother closed her eyes, ready to cry. Something under people's feet sucked them down, something wanted to swallow them. Clara suffered from a nightmare about this, Clara, always so silent, who seemed to float on top of the swamp.

Perhaps all this was her punishment, all the grief, the pain, all the family conflicts, her punishment, because she had blocked the love of Martin and Ella for each other. To forbid love was to forbid life, the forbidding of love engendered death, whatever kind of love, whatever kind of forbidding. Was that it?

Her mind wandered. Mother let herself fall back on the bed, her legs dangling above the floor. One day she'd think about this some more, and then talk with Martin. She'd ask him: Do you think I hurt you?

Some day . . . , she promised herself. When she wasn't so depressed. Now there was a dead boy in the house, and in a few hours the burial. What had the life of that strange boy been like? She had certainly loved him, she had thought those twins beautiful, pure, inaccessible.

For a moment she imagined Carolina's loneliness, the rupture she suffered. No one would pay much attention to this girl, everyone was so twisted up.

Before going to sleep Mother was again struck by the notion she had resisted for so many years, the notion that always assaulted her when weariness left her defenseless.

If Ella would just die, I could finally rest.

A maid was making coffee in the kitchen. It was almost daybreak. Soon everybody would return, disoriented by the fog, thirsty for coffee and news, they would fill the house, they would pass quickly by the casket to take a look at the dead boy.

There was a light on in the room belonging to Carolina, who was sitting on the floor, on the rug.

I have begun to rot, she thought. I can't carry that part around for long, it will contaminate me, his worms will eat my eyes and choke my veins. His soul will drag me to wherever he is. And I'll be just like Ella.

Carolina buried her face in her hands: I'm going to be just like her who stinks like rot in a cave, who stinks like an animal.

She smelled the palms of her hands, her arms, she opened her blouse and lowered her head to try to catch some sign of her body's dissolution.

Then she pressed her hands against her breast. "You're here, my love," she said.

Had Camilo witnessed everything? Was it he leaning against the doorjamb, or had she had an illusion? Carolina felt ravaged. Was this what we had sought? Was this the way we had to go? The experience was so much more intense than she had imagined, it made her crazy. Teetering in convulsions at the edge of the abyss terrified her. And then in the last contraction to feel Death pulling at her womb, to feel its greediness, its impatience.

Carolina recalled what had happened, the fury, the pink blood she later found on the sheets. Was that indecent woman really she, that mare, that naked female demon opening up and burning?

She knew then that she was touching a savage, morbid, distant aspect of Camilo but that she was also losing him forever in the damp, musty body rubbing against hers.

Perhaps it was all a seductive trap set by a demon. They had been used, the three of them, by someone more astute than they, and more lascivious. The Intruder himself, entering her body by force, her immaculate body, saw himself desiring Camilo, like someone desiring his own death, loving Camilo in Carolina, who was merely the passageway. Was that what had happened?

Now it was the cold Lady who possessed Camilo, who had begun to defile him with her obscene touch, who reached Carolina too, through the last remaining fiber that held her to her other part. Life, a serpent eating its own tail, at once beginning and end, masculine and feminine, pleasure and destruction.

Carolina got up with difficulty, her sex still painful. She covered it with her hands in an effort to hide it.

"Can we never go back again?" She buried her fingernails in her arms, scratching her skin, opening bloody gashes. She tore at herself with hatred and pain, she wanted pain, it hurt less than the thought of Camilo rotting.

Then her tension seemed to leave her. She went to the closet, reached inside, pulled out a large pair of scissors.

She raised the scissors to her lips. With her eyes shut she kissed the blades, licking the edges as if they were the lips of a lover. Her mouth tasted blood. The kiss. Who had once surprised her with that sudden, delicious kiss? *Who?*

It didn't matter anymore. It was all a deception, everything, except Death. The waters of truth. Cunning, trickery were useless. Death with its thousand mouths was sucking through the mud at the bottom. There was no resisting it.

Even so, she could not let it take over, she could not give in. Not yet.

She looked at Camilo, infinitely absent Camilo. His sweet breath that she knew so well, where was the wave of his breath rolling now? His hands that had given her strength, that had so often guided her, how could they remain so still when she felt ravaged?

It wasn't possible, he must be somewhere, his heart beating. She pressed her ear to his chest to hear his sounds, his speech. Where was he now?

And his thinking, always connected to hers, it just could not flicker out, where did it shine now?

It was necessary to really concentrate to find Camilo, who had abandoned his own body, now decorated with flowers and candles as if for a party. A betrothal—somewhere Camilo was being unfaithful to her.

In recent months Carolina had noticed that her brother was no longer satisfied living with her. The connection that was perfect for her made him restless, he felt a turbulence that tormented him, that she couldn't understand. There was something outside the bounds of their private love, which had once sustained them. What was it?

Standing in the room, holding the scissors like a flower,

100

she turned her gaze inward, she would discover where Camilo was. She needed his help, to live or to die.

Then, slowly she raised her arms.

Wielding the scissors without a mirror, blindly, determinedly, taking strands of curly hair in one hand, she began to cut. Light glanced off the blades, the clinking steel marked her rhythm. A repetition of the past, of the time she had cut Camilo's hair.

When the twins were still wearing their hair alike, down to their shoulders. When they were thirteen years old. Martin was at Mother's house, he visited her often and saw his children there only. His strange children, who unintentionally mixed him up. After confusing them with each other, Martin got irritated, maybe even frightened, and he asked Clara to get the scissors.

No one moved, no one spoke in the living room turned theater. Camilo standing, Carolina at his side, they hardly glanced at each other.

Martin handed the scissors to his daughter: "You cut your brother's hair, so that he will at least *appear* to be a man."

Camilo had knelt beside her, silent, gazing at her with love illuminating his face. It was a scene of two thirteen-year-old girls acting on the stage of their own, mysterious dimension.

Carolina's hand did not shake.

Now, all alone, she cut away the last sign that distinguished her from Camilo, the last mark of identification. When she had finished, she was the same figure who had knelt in Mother's living room years before, with a delicate head of close-cropped curls. Those burning eyes, what did they see?

She unfolded her arms, she stroked her own body, she clutched herself. From now on pleasure and love would come from within her own walls, where there were no windows or doors, where she was totally alone. To live meant to slide gradually into the wide open mouth of Death, Wind-flower forever sucking, into the gash, the lips.

Had Camilo abandoned her? Had he exchanged her for the final revelation that would be all or nothing? She, Carolina, would have to live with that question. Had she lost him or had she become one with him?

"You must be here, my love," she whispered. That idea intoxicated her like champagne in tall gold glasses, it made her feel as if she were pressing her mouth to her lover's, passing drunken bubbles from mouth to mouth, and cold, pure blood, a single body.

It was like two souls tearing themselves free of the anguish and violence of flesh, sensuality, perfume, and pleasure. After the pain of being separate, now they were, perhaps, a single soul. Lips, gash, mouth, *word*.

IX

Dawn was breaking.

Sitting there alone when the maid arrived with a tray of coffee, Renata and Martin attempted to straighten their clothes and make their hair presentable. They swallowed the coffee quickly and returned the cups, not knowing what to do next.

Martin grimaced, and got up with a groan. It had been a long night, and he still had much to face. More condolences, the burial, and afterwards the return to his small city apartment where he'd lived for the last few years.

Renata fell back into her chair, frozen, she would never leave. Camilo must be arriving on the Island by now, his nocturnal bride had taken him there. The dead, defined forever, remain what we want them to be. We can toss dust and ashes over them, and they will stay quiet to help us cope. As long as we forget to ask: *Where are they?*

If Renata knew the answer, perhaps she could participate in Camilo's new dimension. If there were words.

What could he be trying to say?

She shouldn't look for people to blame, there were only victims. Camilo, Carolina. Martin. What did I give him? I gave nothing to him either. And Martin may have been the only solid thing in my life. I've always needed solid things, and I've always rejected them. Miguel would have been solid, Martin would have supported me, given me strength. But I had to punish myself because something in me could never find order. Who knows if music . . . ? But it's too late now. Who can say that music was not a deception as well?

Perhaps she'd be able to be a mother to Carolina, the survivor. She'd think more about that tomorrow, or the day after. Deep down she knew that one didn't concoct affection. She desperately needed to be able to love, and she didn't know how to love.

Yet she'd spent her life doing what she had to do, devoting herself to her art and paying the price of solitude, giving herself to Martin and causing so many to suffer. And she could change nothing. It was her damnation, her fate.

She rubbed her eyes. Her eyelids were dry as parchment. The picture was still crooked, beautiful, consoling.

Then, at the end of her strength, Renata finally understood.

The boatman was not a man, it was a *woman*. The figure on the prow was she, Camilo's Lover, *Thanatos*. And Thanatos would give herself to him, beneath the shroud.

Renata clasped her hands together, her fingers immobile. In her mind there was not music but peace, almost. The name echoed within her, Thanatos, Thanatos. Was Thanatos really a woman? But maybe that's unimportant. The name . . .

Martin walked over to the big window, opened the shutters, and blinked at the brightness of the day, which had transformed the fog into a sea of cloudy light. The cold air entered the living room, as did the smell of the leaves and the wet ground. Night had ended, but the problems would not. Dead, his son had escaped his desire for love. Where was Camilo? Where had his life gone?

Martin knew that in his love for Renata there was no hope, no sweetness. Every day she would be sucked in further by failure and doubt and her compulsion, which kept her from being happy.

He no longer desired her physically, he was defeated now, and hurt. He loved in her what he could never understand, that strange country which was her soul, there, beautiful and desirable, filled with pain. Walls. She had spent her entire life within herself, unable to get out.

As Martin turned his face toward the cloudy brightness outside, deep in thoughts of his wife, Renata rose from her chair and leaned over. Her son was circling away from her, farther and farther away. Was God the Island? Or the eternal sea?

I betrayed myself when I abandoned music to be unhappy in love. But what is betrayal? Am I not always trading one thing for another because my heart decides that the other is better and so I should seek it instead?

There was no such thing as betrayal. Everything was a constant chaotic pulsation, a search for a meaning in life, because life rushed towards its own end. People dragging themselves through the tunnel, soiling their hands, scratching their faces, filling their mouths with dirt and suffocating their souls. Moments of ecstasy, moments of despair. Only Camilo could know what there was afterwards. *Thanatos*: the answer he was learning, the name.

Now Renata's heart was empty.

She had no more desire to play the piano.

The anguish that had punished her doubly, since with the Angel's death she had given up playing, the urge, the compulsion that moved her, that made her moan like a soul in torment, had also died within her. It was all over.

I am having to be reborn. Another storm, a birth. Pain,

fear, now what will come? Perhaps in the emptiness there will finally be rest.

The two of them, who had once loved each other, were momentarily motionless, Renata absorbed in the silence within herself, Martin still trying to fight, but against whom, against what?

Neither he nor Renata, nobody, except perhaps the dead boy, heard the noise.

In the house somewhere someone was laughing.

The gasping, throaty laughter of an old demon crouched in a corner issued from the end of the corridor upstairs, ricocheted off the walls, rolled hollowly down the steps.

Ella was laughing, she was laughing so much that her enormous body shook, she shut her eyes tight, in a frenzy she pressed the pillow with her head again and again.

The sick heart of the house was exploding. Like the excrement, rotten leaves, and worms an animal accumulates in his cave, the accumulated pain, the consciousness repugnant to itself, and the repulsion of others began to explode.

Everywhere, under the beds, in the corners where no one cleaned, behind the furniture and the curtains, balls of dust and great spider webs were beginning to move.

The breath of hell blew up Renata's skirt, who held it down with both hands. Where was it coming from? It whistled across Martin's back, Martin turned around, startled, puzzled. The cold air came from inside the house, an exhalation, the Word, the Name?

Then the laughter went out the window and swept through the spirals of fog in the garden. Over the black treetops the pulsations of a new day forced light into the thick fog, and the light struck the living room, where the dead boy embraced his Lover as they docked.